NEW YORK REVIEW BOOKS
CLASSICS

T0286647

BERLIN STORIES

ROBERT WALSER (1878–1956) was born into a German-speaking family in Biel, Switzerland. He left school at fourteen and led a wandering, precarious existence while writing his poems, novels, and vast numbers of the "prose pieces" that became his hallmark. In 1933 he was confined to a sanatorium, which marked the end of his writing career. Among Walser's works available in English are *Jakob von Gunten* (available as an NYRB classic), *The Tanners*, *Microscripts*, *The Assistant*, *The Robber*, *Masquerade and Other Stories*, and *Speaking to the Rose: Writings, 1912–1932*.

JOCHEN GREVEN is the author of the first German-language PhD dissertation on Robert Walser and the editor of Walser's collected works in German. As a graduate student in the 1950s, he recognized that Walser's "microscripts" (manuscript pages covered with tiny handwriting discovered after Walser's death) were not written in secret code but were in fact literary texts in standard German. Greven has devoted more than fifty years to studying and editing Walser's work.

SUSAN BERNOFSKY is the translator of six books by Robert Walser as well as works by Jenny Erpenbeck, Yoko Tawada, Hermann Hesse, Gregor von Rezzori, and others. The current chair of the PEN Translation Committee, she teaches in the MFA Program in Creative Writing and Literary Translation at Queens College (CUNY) and is at work on a biography of Walser.

BERLIN STORIES

ROBERT WALSER

Edited by
JOCHEN GREVEN

Translated from the German by
SUSAN BERNOFSKY
and others

NEW YORK REVIEW BOOKS

New York

THIS IS A NEW YORK REVIEW BOOK
PUBLISHED BY THE NEW YORK REVIEW OF BOOKS
207 East 32nd Street, New York, NY 10016
www.nyrb.com

Originally published by Suhrkamp Verlag in German as *Robert Walser: Berlin gibt immer den Ton an*

The following stories have previously appeared in the present translation in slightly different form: "Frau Scheer" in *M Review/Habit*; "Kutsch," "Cowshed," and "Do You Know Meier?" in *Agni*; "Full" in *Asymptote*; "In the Electric Tram" and "Fabulous" in *Green Mountains Review*; "Good Morning, Giantess!," "Market," "Aschinger," and "Mountain Halls" in *Masquerade and Other Stories*, pp. 23–25, 30–36, © 1990 by The Johns Hopkins University Press, reprinted with permission of The Johns Hopkins University Press; "The Park" in *The Review of Contemporary Fiction: Robert Walser* (Spring, 1992); "Flower Days," "Frau Wilke," and "The Little Berliner" from *Selected Stories* by Robert Walser, translated by Christopher Middleton and others, with an introduction by Susan Sontag, translation and compilation © 1982 by Farrar, Straus and Giroux, Inc., reprinted by permission of Farrar, Straus and Giroux, LLC. and Carcanet Press Ltd..

Library of Congress Cataloging-in-Publication Data
Walser, Robert, 1878–1956.
 Berlin stories / by Robert Walser ; translated and with an introduction by Susan Bernofsky ; edited by Jochen Greven.
   p. cm. — (New York review books classics)
 ISBN 978-1-59017-454-8 (alk. paper)
1. Berlin (Germany)—Fiction. I. Bernofsky, Susan. II. Greven, Jochen. III. Title.
PT2647.A64A2 2011
833'.912—dc22

                    2011013388

ISBN 978-1-59017-454-8
Available as an electronic book; ISBN 978-1-59017-473-9

Printed in the United States of America on acid-free paper.
10 9 8

CONTENTS

INTRODUCTION

THE YOUNG Swiss writer Robert Walser moved to Berlin in the summer of 1905, at the age of twenty-seven. He'd just published his first book, the outlines of a successful literary career were beginning to unfold before him, and the moment seemed ripe to leave behind the relative peace and safety of his native land for the stimulation and excitement of the German capital. Then as now, Berlin was the destination of choice for young German-speaking writers eager to tap into the pulse of the avant-garde, and his brother Karl, who'd made the move several years before and quickly established himself as the city's foremost stage-set designer, had been encouraging Robert to join him. Karl's celebrity secured his younger brother entry into the most exclusive artistic circles, where he met actresses and painters, theater directors and publishers, some of whom took an interest in him.

Berlin in those days was hopping. The city had undergone a period of intense growth in the final decades of the nineteenth century—its population swelled to two million by 1900—and was the site of one of the liveliest high societies in Europe. While factories had bred slums in the city's northern and eastern districts, the elegance of several of its neighborhoods rivaled that of Paris, though Berlin was more densely packed than the French capital with its brightly lit Grands Boulevards. But Berlin had splendid avenues of its own: Unter den Linden to the east, lined with a double row of the linden trees it was named for, and the swank Kurfürstendamm to the west, as well as a capacious park called Tiergarten, a former hunting ground full of well-tended serpentine paths for Sunday strolls. Potsdamer Platz, Berlin's busiest intersection (and the one Curt Bois reminisces about in Wim Wenders's *Wings of Desire*), was a tangle of pedestrians, horse-drawn carriages, automobiles, omnibuses, and electric streetcars; by 1908, thirty-five streetcar lines stopped here. Subway cars began to run in 1902, two years earlier than in New York, and people hurried in and out of newfangled restaurants designed for rapid service, like those of the Aschinger chain Walser writes about in two of the stories included here. At Aschinger, one ate standing up, and unlimited free rolls were served to anyone buying a beer. The city's headlong dive into modernity soon became its trademark. Walser's acquaintance Walther Rathenau—who later would become foreign minister of Germany—quipped that Berlin's oldest palaces dated to the early Wilhelmine period, i.e., the late nineteenth century, and dubbed Berlin "Parvenupolis."

Among Berlin's would-be parvenus were any number of young artists. The city appeared to reward youthful rebelliousness. Its philharmonic orchestra was formed in 1882 when a group of musicians broke away from the ensemble at a music hall that provided military-band-style entertainment along with ham sandwiches; they moved into a renovated roller-skating rink and soon began performing a repertoire that included Brahms, Wagner, and the young composers Felix Weingartner and Richard Strauss. In the visual arts it was no different: a group of artists removed themselves from the official Association of Berlin Artists in 1892 after the association succumbed to pressure from Kaiser Wilhelm to shut down a show featuring Edvard Munch. The Berlin Secession, as this group soon dubbed itself, quickly rose to prominence and included such luminaries as Max Liebermann, Lovis Corinth, Max Beckmann, Max Slevogt, Walter Leistikow—and Karl Walser. Robert Walser himself served as secretary to the Secession for several months in 1907, as he reminisces in his story "The Secretary." There were theaters everywhere (their number swelled to thirty-seven by the 1920s), not to mention the many variety shows and cabarets for which the city was to become famous.

Walser had been to Berlin before, twice in fact: in 1897 as a lad of nineteen, and again in 1902; but each time he had fled back to Zurich after only a few weeks, in large part because he felt he would be unable to support himself as a writer in the German metropolis. In 1905, though, he held out for nearly three months before traveling back to Zurich, and after only a few weeks there found himself missing the bustle and excitement of the city so much that he returned, overflowing with newfound optimism. In a note to a friend in Biel, he wrote, "I'm about to write so much that Hesse and Co. will be terrified." Berlin was to be his home for more than seven years, and the books he wrote here firmly established him as one of the most singular and original voices of European modernism.

For Karl Walser, 1905 was a watershed year. He had recently begun a series of collaborations with the era's most famous theater director, Max Reinhardt, and in January they put on *A Midsummer Night's Dream* together at the Theater am Schiffbauerdamm. In November a grand new opera house, the Komische Oper, opened its doors with a Reinhardt production that one prominent reviewer dubbed "The Tales of Hoffmann—A Walser Dream." Karl's stage sets were fanciful, mysterious, and full of romantic gardenscapes and hanging trees, images that also appeared in the paintings he exhibited at Berlin Secession shows. That year he drew the cover illustration for Christian Morgenstern's collection of humorous poems *Gallows Songs*, and the book became a surprise best seller. In the middle of the summer, just as Robert Walser was on his way back from Switzerland, Karl packed up his paints and brushes and set off for the elegant neighborhood of Grunewald at the wooded edge of town, where Samuel Fischer, one of the most powerful publishers in Germany, had hired him to paint a series of frescoes in his freshly renovated villa.

For Robert Walser, his brother's heady rise to fame and fortune must have been as overwhelming as it was unexpected. After all, his brother—only one year his senior—had himself arrived in Berlin penniless, an unknown provincial with a thick accent and inexperienced in the rituals of high society. But while Karl was able to swim with ease in the waters of Berlin's beau monde, it soon became clear that his social circles were only partially permeable to the younger

Walser brother. Robert, who was living as a guest in Karl's apartment in the tony Charlottenburg district, soon developed a reputation as a big drinker and a sometimes too enthusiastic prankster. He walked up to Hugo von Hofmannsthal in a restaurant and asked the celebrated dramatist, "Can't you forget for a bit that you're famous?" Robert and Karl once teased Franz Wedekind—for whose *Spring Awakening* Karl designed the sets—so persistently that Wedekind fled a dinner party to escape them, only to get stuck in a café's revolving door, where the brothers cornered him once more, shouting "Schafskopf!" (muttonhead) as he whirled past.

In a letter to their sister Fanny, Robert describes his attempt to assimilate to his elegant new surroundings and social life:

> So little soup was served that afterwards the vegetables and the roast meat were doubly appealing. After lunch I passed the hours gazing at myself in four beautiful mirrors that were hung up in the blue living room, and yet came no closer to making sense of myself—on the contrary, I became stupider and stupider. Then I went calling and always returned home famished. You had to take the train, and that was splendid. I grew accustomed to hackney cabs, waiters, and refined ladies. I wore an elegant, long, black, close-fitting frock coat, a vest, silver-blue in color, trousers that didn't fit so well, a tall hat and a pair of gloves balled up in my hands. I looked magnificent, for a coat like this makes one a human being. But I resolved to remain an honest man, and so I threw off these dainty coverings. I packed my miserable carpenter's bag and sailed off.

As fond as he may have been of that coat—no doubt borrowed—which his brother's roomful of mirrors encouraged him to admire, he seems not to have considered it anything more than a costume by means of which he might blend in. The camouflage seems not to have worked: Karl once received a dinner invitation that instructed him to bring his brother along "only if he isn't too hungry."

For reasons that have never become as clear as we might like, Walser decided several months after his arrival in Berlin to enroll in a monthlong course of study at the Herrschaftliche Dienerschule (Aristocratic Servants School) located at Wilhelmstrasse 28, not far from Unter den Linden and the fancy shopping street Friedrichstrasse. The curriculum at this school included such topics as waiting at table, cleaning, carving roasts, keeping the household accounts, napkin folding, handling "nervous persons," and massage. By 1911, the list was updated to include instruction in the use of electrical lights, central heating, and telephones.

Almost nothing is known about Walser's experiences at the servants' school. Its pupils were adults, and Walser remembered some of them decades later as possessed of "the delicacy of page boys." The school also appears, radically transformed, as the boys' school "Institute Benjamenta" in Walser's 1909 novel *Jakob von Gunten*. All that is directly recognizable is the basic structure of the curriculum: Jakob notes that the lessons are both "practical" and "theoretical" in nature. After Walser graduated, he served for the length of one winter as an assistant butler at a count's castle in upper Silesia, an adventure that goes strikingly unrecorded in the stories dating from this period. Walser did not write about this interlude until more than a decade later, in the 1917 story "Tobold."[1]

In any case, Walser soon returned to Berlin, where he worked odd jobs; lived in part with his brother, in part in a series of furnished rooms; and wrote a large number of short prose texts for publication in literary magazines as well as the feuilleton sections of newspapers, including the *Berliner Tageblatt*, the *Vossische Zeitung*, and the *Frankfurter Zeitung*. While we tend to call these texts "stories," Walser himself described them as "prose pieces"; this hybrid of story and essay remained his genre of choice for most of his writing career. He also published three novels: *The Tanners* (1907), *The Assistant* (1908),

---

1. "Tobold (II)"—the roman numeral indicates that this is the second story Walser wrote with this title—appears in my translation in *Masquerade and Other Stories* (Baltimore: The Johns Hopkins University Press, 1990), 80–100.

and *Jakob von Gunten*. Only the last of the three is set in Berlin—though even in this book the city goes unnamed. But his short prose texts offer clear evidence of his love affair with the metropolis.

The stories collected in this volume were chosen by Walser's long-time German editor Jochen Greven, mostly from among the 120 or so pieces Walser wrote during his Berlin years. Greven has arranged the book as a four-part symphony, the final movement of which comprises texts that look back on Walser's Berlin experiences at a remove of several years. And although Walser wrote stories about a great range of subjects while living in Berlin (including the beautiful historical fictions "Kleist in Thun" and "The Battle of Sempach"),[2] Greven has—quite appropriately—limited his selection to stories that take Berlin as their subject matter. From them a portrait of the city emerges that speaks of bustling streets, technology-fueled haste, social and artistic striving, and a certain melting-pot quality seen above all in the public parks where many levels of society intersect.

The Berlin of these stories is a land of artistic possibility, where poets produce immortal works, virtuoso actors stun their audiences, and painters find inspiration. The narrators often seem to be bursting with an openhearted enthusiasm that at times can sound naïve. But we are also shown a handful of failures: spurned lovers, unsuccessful artists, and people whose behavior causes them to live as outcasts among their neighbors. "The metropolitan artist," Walser writes in "Berlin and the Artist," "has no dearth of opportunities to see and speak to no one at all. All he has to do is make himself unpopular among certain arbiters of taste or else consistently fixate on failures, and in no time he'll have sunk into the most splendid, most blossoming of abandonments."

A number of the stories in this collection are devoted to the theater, which Walser knew not only through his brother but through his own early aspirations. He'd once dreamed of becoming an actor,

---

2. "Kleist in Thun" can be found, in Christopher Middleton's translation, in *Selected Stories of Robert Walser* (NYRB Classics, 2002), 17–26. "The Battle of Sempach," in my own translation, appears in *Masquerade and Other Stories*, 37–42.

and as a seventeen-year-old had traveled to Stuttgart, where his brother was living, and had an audience with an actor he hoped would mentor him. Nothing came of it. Gertrud Eysoldt, the actress mentioned in passing in "Four Amusements," was at the time the star of Stuttgart's Königliches Hoftheater and later worked with Max Reinhardt in Berlin. Walser's favorite playwrights included Friedrich Schiller (author of *The Robbers*) and Heinrich von Kleist, whose final play, *Prince Friedrich of Homburg*, is quoted in both "A Person Possessed of Curiosity" and "Portrait Sketch." While living in Berlin, Walser attended not only the grand theaters where his brother designed the stage sets but also—as we see in several stories here—the shabby little variety shows that offered entertainment to working-class Berliners.

Walser's view of the "capital" and "metropolis" is consistently a modest one. He writes far less of the grand soirées he witnessed than of much humbler experiences of city life—in keeping with W. G. Sebald's view of him as a "clairvoyant of the small." The chirpy delight some of his narrators take in the city's hum and bustle also reflects his own status as an outsider who enjoys blending in with the crowd. He occasionally thematizes his Swissness, for the most part humorously. In "Something About the Railway" he describes a waitress as being clad in *Oberländertracht*—the traditional costume worn in the Oberland or upcountry region outside Bern—a bit of cultural specificity likely to have eluded his fellow Berliners. His funniest allusion to Swissness is lamentably invisible in translation; it comes at the end of "What Became of Me" when, after poking fun at his countryman Ernst Zahn—author of sentimental Alpine romances —for exploiting his nationality for commercial success, Walser concludes by praising the Berliners as *schaffig*, using a Swiss dialect word for "hardworking." Walser's playfulness also comes out in his stories about his writer colleague Kutsch (a name charmingly close to "kitsch")—this being a pseudonym under which Walser himself published several stories. And the humor of his sketch "Mountain Halls"—a description of a variety show located on Unter den Linden—made this piece a favorite of Kafka's. Max Brod describes

Kafka collapsing in paroxysms of laughter while reading the story aloud.

The final stories in this collection allude more or less obliquely to the difficulties Walser experienced near the end of his Berlin years. While his three novels had been well-received by reviewers and other writers, not one of them sold well—a circumstance he found highly discouraging. Toward the end of his time in Berlin, he suffered a psychological crisis accompanied by severe writer's block that plagued him for a good two years. Eventually he was able to write again thanks to the "microscript" technique he developed for composing his rough drafts. This technique, which he would continue to rely on for the rest of his literary career, is described in detail in my introduction to Robert Walser, *Microscripts* (New Directions/ Christine Burgin, 2010). The effect of this crisis can be seen in the relative dearth of texts from 1910 and 1911, though by 1912 Walser was back to writing at his usual level of productivity. It would be years, however, before he wrote another novel. In March 1913, after the death of the landlady described in the story "Frau Scheer," he returned to Switzerland for good.

Some of the stories in this collection previously appeared—in translations by Christopher Middleton in two cases, Harriett Watts in one—in the 1982 collection *Selected Stories of Robert Walser*. In another case I inadvertently retranslated a story, "*The Tanners*," that Middleton had published under a different title in his lovely Walser collection *Speaking to the Rose: Writings 1912–1932* (University of Nebraska Press, 2005); I decided to let my translation stand so that the curious reader will have two versions to compare. Middleton's translations of Walser, the earliest of which date to the mid-1950s, are spirited and alive in every sentence, displaying the depth and range of Walser's imagination. I have done my best, in my own translations, to re-create the playful wit and profound sagacity that speak from every page of Walser's prose.

—SUSAN BERNOFSKY
New York, September 2011

THE CITY STREETS

GOOD MORNING, GIANTESS!

IT'S AS if a giantess were shaking her curls and sticking one leg out of bed when—early in the morning, before even the electric trams are running, and driven by some duty or other—you venture out into the metropolis. Cold and white the streets lie there, like outstretched human arms; you trot along, rubbing your hands, and watch people coming out of the gates and doorways of their buildings, as though some impatient monster were spewing out warm, flaming saliva. You encounter eyes as you walk along like this: girls' eyes and the eyes of men, mirthless and gay; legs are trotting behind and before you, and you too are legging along as best you can, gazing with your own eyes, glancing the same glances as everyone else. And each breast bears some somnolent secret, each head is haunted by some melancholy or inspiring thought. Splendid, splendid. So it is a cold morning—half sunny, half gray—and many, many people are still snug in their beds: revelers who've lived and adventured their way though the entire night and half the morning, refined persons who make it a habit to arise late, lazy dogs that wake up, give a yawn, and go back to snoring twenty times in a row, graybeards and invalids who can no longer get up at all or only with difficulty, women who have loved, artists who say to themselves: Get up early? What rubbish!, the children of wealthy, beautiful parents—fabulously coddled, sheltered creatures who go on sleeping in their own little rooms behind snow-white curtains, their little mouths open, immersed in fairy-tale dreams until nine, ten, or eleven o'clock. At such an early hour of morning, the wild maze of streets is all a-skitter and a-scurry with if not stage-set painters, then at least paperhangers, clerks who copy addresses, paltry insignificant middlemen, as well as persons intending to catch an early train to Vienna, Munich, Paris, or Hamburg, for the most part people of no significance, girls from all possible spheres of employment, working girls, in other words. Anyone observing this hubbub will have no choice but to declare it exceptional. He then walks along like this and is almost taken up by a compulsion to join in this running, this gasping haste, swinging his arms to and fro; the bustle and activity are just so contagious— the way a beautiful smile can be contagious. Well no, not like that. The early morning is something completely different. It flings, for example, one last pair of grimily clad night owls with loathsomely red-painted faces out of their barrooms and onto the blinding, dusty white street where they loiter, stupefied, for quite some time with their crooked sticks over their shoulders, annoying the passersby. How the drunken night shines forth from their sullied eyes! On- ward, onward. That blue-eyed marvel, the early morning, has no time to waste on drunkards. It has a thousand shimmering threads with which it draws you on; it pushes you from behind and smiles coaxingly from the front. You glance up to where a whitish, veiled sky is letting a few scraps of blue peek out; behind you, to gaze after a person who interests you; beside you, at an opulent portal behind which a regal palace morosely, elegantly towers up. Statues beckon you from gardens and parks; still you keep on walking, giving every- thing a passing glance: things in motion and things fixed in place, hackney cabs indolently lumbering along, the electric tram just now starting its run, from whose windows human eyes regard you, a con- stable's idiotic helmet, a person with tattered shoes and trousers, a person of no doubt erstwhile high standing who is sweeping the street in a top hat and fur coat; you glance at everything, just as you yourself are a fleeting target for all these other eyes. That is what is so miraculous about a city: that each person's bearing and conduct van- ishes among all these thousand types, that everything is observed in passing, judgments made in an instant, and forgetting a matter of course. Past. What's gone past? A façade from the Empire period? Where? Back there? Could a person possibly decide to turn around once more so as to give the old architecture a supplementary glance? Good heavens, no. Onward, onward. The chest expands, the giantess Metropolis has just, with the most voluptuous leisureliness, pulled on her sun-shimmery chemise. A giantess like this doesn't dress so quickly; but each of her beautiful, huge motions is fragrant and steams and pounds and peals. Hackney cabs with American luggage on top clatter past mangling the language. Now you are walking in the park; the motionless canals are still covered in gray ice, the meadows make you shiver, the slender, thin, bare trees chase you swiftly on with their icily quivering appearance; carts are being pushed, two stately carriages from the coach house of some person or other of official standing sweep past, each bearing two coachmen and a lackey; always there is something, and each time you wish to observe this something more closely, it's already gone. Naturally you have a large number of thoughts during your one-hour march, you are a poet and can practice your art without removing your hands from the pockets of your—let us hope—respectable overcoat, you are a painter and perhaps have already finished five pictures during your morning stroll. You are an aristocrat, hero, lion tamer, Socialist, African explorer, ballet dancer, gymnast, or bartender, and you've fleetingly dreamed just now of having been introduced to the Kaiser. He climbed down from his throne and drew you into a friendly half-hour chat in which his lady the Empress may also have taken part. In your thoughts you rode the metropolitan railway, tore the laurel wreath from Dernburg's brow, got married and settled down in a village in Switzerland, wrote a stage-worthy drama—jolly, jolly, onward, hey there, what? Could that be . . . ? Indeed, then you ran into your colleague Kitsch, and the two of you went home together for a cup of chocolate.

1907

THE PARK

SOLDIERS on duty sit on a bench beside the entryway, I go in, dry, fallen leaves fly and swirl and sweep and tumble toward me. This is exceptionally amusing and at the same time contemplative; the lively is always more contemplative than what is dead and sad. Park air welcomes me; the many thousand green leaves of the lofty trees are lips that wish me good morning: So you're up already too? Indeed, yes, I'm surprised myself. A park like this resembles a large, silent, isolated room. In fact it's always Sunday in a park, by the way, for it's always a bit melancholy, and the melancholy stirs up vivid memories of home, and Sunday is something that only ever existed at home, where you were a child. Sundays have something parental and childish about them. I walk on beneath the tall, beautiful trees, how softly and amicably they rustle, a girl is sitting all alone upon a bench, poking the ground with her parasol, her pretty head bowed, absorbed in thought. What might she be thinking? Would she like to make an acquaintance? A long, pale-green avenue opens up, here and there a person walks toward me, the benches meanwhile are only rather sparsely populated. How the sun does like to shine, for no reason at all. It kisses the trees and the water of the artificially constructed lake; I examine an old railing and laugh because it pleases me. Nowadays it's fashionable to pause before old iron railings to admire their sturdy, delicate workmanship, which is a bit silly. Onward. Suddenly an acquaintance is standing before me: Kutsch, the writer, who fails to recognize me although I call out a friendly greeting. What's wrong with him? By the way, I'd thought all this time he'd gone off to the African colonies. I hurry up to him, but all at

6

once he vanishes; indeed, this was only a foolish delusion on my part: the spot beneath the tall oak tree where I thought I saw him is empty. A bridge! How the water glistens and shimmers in the sun, so enchantingly. But there's no one rowing here, which makes the lake appear drowsy, it's as if it were only a painted lake. Young people arrive. Strange, the way we look into each other's eyes on a Sunday afternoon like this, as if we had something to say to one another, but we have nothing at all to say, we say to ourselves. A small, charmingly slender castle rises before me between the trees in the blue-and-white air. Who might have lived here? Perhaps someone's mistress? I hope so, it's an appealing thought. This place may once have swarmed with high and the highest nobility, hackney cabs and carriages and servants in green-and-blue livery. How deserted and neglected this stately edifice appears! Thank God no one notices, for if an architect were to come and renovate it with the help of his intellectual spectacles—with your permission, I'll swallow this notion unpondered. What has become of us as a people that we can possess the beautiful only in dreams. An old woman and an old man sit there, I walk past and also pass a girl who is reading; no use trying to begin a romance with the words: "What are you reading, miss?" I am walking rather quickly, then suddenly stop: how beautiful and quiet such a park is, it transports you to the most distant landscapes, you find yourself in England or Silesia, you're lord of the manor and nothing at all. The most beautiful thing is when you seem not to be conscious of the beauty and merely exist as do other things as well. I gaze down for a while at the silent, half-green river. Everything, by the way, is so green, and so gray, which actually is a color for slumber, for closing one's eyes. In the distance, ringed with leaves, one sees the bluish dress of a seated lady. Cigarette smoking isn't permitted here either. A girl laughs brightly, strolling between two young gentlemen, one of whom has his arm around her. Once more a view down an avenue of trees, how beautiful, how quiet, how strange. An old woman comes toward me, her delicate, pale face framed in black, these old, clever eyes. In all honesty, I find it magnificent when a solitary old woman walks down a green avenue. I reach a bed of flowers and other vegetation where, on a pretty, shady bench, sits a Jew. Should it have been a Teuton, would that be better? A small statue stands surrounded by flowers in a circular bed, I walk slowly around its edge, and now the reading girl appears once more, she's reading as she walks, studying French under her breath. This marvelous boredom that is in all things, this sunny seclusion, this halfheartedness and drowsiness beneath the green, this melancholy, these legs, whose legs, mine? Yes. I'm too indolent to make observations, I gaze down at my legs and march onward. I mean it: Sundays only exist around the family table and on family walks. The single adult person is deprived of this pleasure, he might as well, like Kutsch, set off for Africa at a moment's notice. Besides, what a loss it is to have turned twenty-five. There are compensations, but at present I want nothing to do with them. I'm on the street now, smoking, and step into a respectable pub, and here I am at once master of my surroundings. Beautiful park, I think, beautiful park.

1907

FRIEDRICHSTRASSE

UP ABOVE is a narrow strip of sky, and the smooth, dark ground below looks as if it's been polished by human destinies. The buildings to either side rise boldly, daintily, and fantastically into architectural heights. The air quivers and startles with worldly life. All the way up to the rooftops, and even above, advertisements float and hang. The large lettering is quite conspicuous. And always people are walking here. Never in all the time this street has existed has life stopped circulating here. This is the very heart, the ceaselessly respiring breast of metropolitan life. It is a place of deep inhalations and mighty exhalations, as if life itself felt disagreeably constricted by its own pace and course. Here is the wellspring, the brook, the stream, the river, and the sea of motion. Never do the movement and commotion here fully die out, and just as life is about to cease at the upper end of the street, it starts up again at the bottom. Work and pleasure, vices and wholesome drives, striving and idleness, nobility and malice, love and hate, ardent and scornful natures, the colorful and the simple, poverty and wealth all shimmer, glisten, dally, daydream, rush, and stumble here frenetically and yet also helplessly. A fetter unlike any other restrains and subdues passions here, and countless allurements lead straightaway to appealing temptations, such that failure's sleeve cannot help but brush against the back of gratified desires and insatiability is inevitably left to gaze with smoldering eyes into the wise, peaceful eyes of a person who finds satiation within himself. There are gaping chasms here, and one sees the rule and reign—to the point of utter impropriety, which no thinking person should take amiss—of opposites, indescribable contradictions. Vehicles keep

9

edging past human bodies, heads and hands, and on their open decks and in their hollow interiors sit people, tightly squeezed in and subjugated, who have some reason to be sitting, squeezing, pressing, and riding either here inside or up on top. Every last silly little thing has its unspeakably swift justification, its good clever grounds. Every foolishness here is ennobled and sanctified by the obvious difficulty of life. Every motion has its meaning, every sound here has practical cause, and from every smile, every gesture, every word a strangely charming staidness and respectability approvingly peeks out. Here one approves of everything, because every individual, compelled by the constraints of the hobbled traffic, has no choice but to approve without hesitation all he hears and sees. No one seems to have the desire to disapprove, the time to dislike, or the right to demur, for here—and this is what's so marvelous—everyone feels obligated in a light, helpful way, tidily obligated as it were. Every beggar, rogue, monster, etc. counts here as a fellow human being and must, for the time being, amid the general press, push, and shove, be tolerated as part of the collectivity. Ah, this is the homeland of the wretched, the little man, no the littlest one, the one who has already been dishonored somewhere and somewhen; here, here tolerance reigns, as no one wishes to spend and waste his time on impatience and displeasure. This is the place of peaceful walks embarked on in the sunshine as if upon a remote, silent mountain meadow, and when the lamplight is shimmering you stroll elegantly about as in a fairy tale filled with magical arts and spells. It's wonderful how ceaseless and incessant the twofold stream of people on the sidewalks is, like a viscous, shimmering, profoundly meaningful body of water, and how splendid it is the way torments are overcome here, wounds concealed, dreams fettered, carnal appetites reined in, joys suppressed, and desires chastened, since all are compelled to be considerate, considerate, and once more lovingly and respectfully considerate. Where a human being finds himself in such proximity to human beings, the concept *neighbor* takes on a genuinely practical, comprehensible, and swiftly grasped meaning, and no one should have the gall to laugh too loudly, devote himself too assiduously to his personal difficulties or insist on concluding business matters too hastily, and yet: what a ravishing, beguiling haste can be seen in all this ostensible packed-in-ness and sober-mindedness. The sun shines here upon countless heads in a single hour, the rain dampens and drenches a ground that is anointed, as it were, with comedies and tragedies, and in the evening, ah, when it begins to grow dark and the lamps are lit, a curtain slowly rises to reveal a play that is always sumptuously full of the same habits, acts of lechery, and occurrences. The siren Pleasure then begins to sing her divinely enticing, heavenly notes, and souls burst asunder amid all these vibrating wants and dissatisfactions, and a disgorging of money then commences that baffles the modest, clever understanding and can scarcely be envisioned, even with effort, by the poetic imagination. A bodily dream rising and falling with voluptuous breath then descends upon the street, and everything races, races, races with uncertain step in pursuit of this all-encompassing dream.

1907

MARKET

A WEEKLY market is something bright, lively, sumptuous, and gay. Through the broad streets that are usually so still stretch two long rows of stands, interrupted by gaps, where lies and hangs everything that households and families require for their daily needs. The sun that in these parts can usually lie about haughtily and idly is now compelled to leap and glint, to flail about, as it were, for every mobile thing here present, every object, every hat, apron, pot, sausage, absolutely everything wants to be given a sparkle. Sausages bathed in sunshine look so splendid. The meat shows off in all its glory, proud and purple, on the hooks from which it hangs. Vegetables are greening and laughing, oranges jesting in stunning golden profusion, fish swimming about in wide tubs of water. You stand like this, and then you take a step. You take ... It's not so terribly important whether the planned, ventured, and executed step is indeed an actual one. This joyful, simple life—how unpretentiously attractive it is, with what middle-class domesticity it laughs at you. And then the sky with its top-notch, first-rate blue. First-rate! One wouldn't want to go so far as to employ the word "sweet." Where poesy can be felt, poetic flights are superfluous. "Three urnges fur a grosch'n." So tell me, mister, could it be you've uttered these words once before? What a selection of splendid, plump women! Coarse human figures make us think of the soil, of country weals and country woes, of God himself, who surely doesn't have so exaggeratedly handsome a physique either. God is the opposite of Rodin. How enchanting this is: being permitted to take a bit of pleasure in something rustic, even only a grosch'n's worth. Fresh eggs, country ham, country and city liverwurst! I have to admit: I do like standing and scallywagging about in the proximity of tempting comestibles. Again I am reminded of the most vivid ephemeralities, and what is alive is dearer to me than the immortal. Flowers here, crockery over there, and right beside it cheese: Swiss, Tilsiter, Dutch, Harzer, with the accompanying odors. If you gaze off now into the distance, hundreds of subjects for landscape paintings come into view; if you look down, you discern apple peels and nut shells, scraps of meat, bits of paper, half and whole international newspapers, a trouser button, a garter. If you look straight up, there's a sky, and if you glance right in front of you, the face of an average person—though we don't speak of average days and nights or an average nature. But isn't the average actually what is solidest and best? I have no use for days or weeks of genius, or an extraordinary Lord God. What is mobile is always the most just. —And how prettily farmwives can look at you. With what odd, quiet gestures they turn this way and that. The market always leaves behind an inkling of country life in this city neighborhood, as if to shake it out of its monotonous pride. How lovely it is that all these wares are lying out in the fresh open air. Boys buy themselves warm sausages and have mustard spread up and down their entire juicy lengths so as to devour them skillfully on the spot. Eating seems so appropriate beneath this lofty blue sky. How enchanting these voluptuous bunches of cauliflower look to me. I shall compare them (somewhat reluctantly) to firm female breasts. The comparison is impertinent if it doesn't work. So many women all around one. But the market, I see, is now coming to an end. Time to pack up shop. Fruit is raked into baskets. Kippers and sprats are stowed away, stalls dismantled. The throng has moved on. Soon the street will have recaptured its former appearance. Adieu, colors. Adieu, all you various things. Adieu, you sprinkling of sounds, scents, motions, footsteps, and lights. By the way, I've struck a bargain for a pound of walnuts. So now I can go trotting home to my apartment full of wee-wee and waa-waa, children's cries. I like to eat just about everything, but when I eat nuts I'm truly happy.

1908

ASCHINGER

A LAGER please! The tap man's known me for ages. I gaze at the filled glass a moment, take it by the handle with two fingers, and casually carry it to one of the round tables supplied with forks, knives, rolls, vinegar, and oil. I place the sweating glass in an orderly fashion upon the felt coaster and consider whether or not to fetch myself something to eat. This food-thought propels me to the blue-and-white-striped cold-cuts damsel. I have this lady serve me a plate of assorted open-face sandwiches and, thus enriched, trot rather indolently back to my seat. Neither fork nor knife do I use, just the mustard spoon, with which I paint my sandwiches brown before inserting them so cozily into my mouth that it is perhaps tranquillity itself to witness this. Another lager please! At Aschinger, you quickly adopt a familiar food-and-drink tone of voice; after a certain amount of time there, a person can't help talking just like Wassmann at the Deutsches Theater. Once you have your fist around your second or third glass of beer, you're generally driven to engage in all manner of observations. It is imperative to note with precision how the Berliners eat. They stand up as they do so, but take their own sweet time about it. It's a myth that in Berlin people only bustle, whizz, and trot about. People here have a nearly comical understanding of how to let time flow by; after all, they're only human. It's a sincere pleasure to watch people fishing for sausage-laden rolls and Italian salads. The payment is extracted mostly from vest pockets, almost always just a matter of small change. Now I've rolled myself a cigarette, which I light at the gas flame beneath its green glass shield. How well I know it, this glass, and the brass chain to pull on. Famished and satiated individuals are constantly swarming in and out. The dissatisfied quickly find satisfaction at the beer spring and the warm sausage tower, and the satiated dash out again into the mercantile air, each generally with a briefcase beneath his arm, a letter in his pocket, an assignment in his brain, firm plans in his skull, and in his open palm a watch that says the time has come. In the round tower at the center of the room reigns a young queen, the sovereign of the sausages and potato salad—she's a bit bored up there in her quiver-like surrounds. An elegant lady enters and with two fingers skewers a roll spread with caviar; at once I bring myself to her notice, but in such a way as if being noticed were of no concern to me at all. Meanwhile I've found time to lay hands on another beer. The elegant lady is somewhat hesitant to bite into the caviar marvel; of course I immediately assume it to be on my account and none other that she is no longer fully in control of her masticatory senses. Delusions are so easy and so agreeable. Outside on the square is a racket no one really hears: a tumult of carriages, people, automobiles, newspaper hawkers, electric trams, handcarts, and bicycles that no one ever really sees either. It's almost unseemly to think of wanting to hear and see all these things, you're not new in town. The elegantly curved bodice that was just nibbling bread now quits the Aschinger. How much longer am I planning on sitting here anyhow? The tap boys are enjoying a calm moment, but not for long, for here they come rolling in again from out-of-doors to throw themselves thirstily upon the bubbling spring. Eaters observe others who are similarly working their jaws. While one person's mouth is full, his eyes can simultaneously behold a neighbor occupied with popping it in. And they don't even laugh; even I don't. Since arriving in Berlin, I've lost the habit of finding humanity laughable. At this point, by the way, I myself request another edible wonder: a plank of bread bearing a sleeping sardine upon a bedsheet of butter, so enchanting a vision that I toss the whole spectacle down my open revolving stage of a gullet. Is such a thing laughable? By no means. Well, then. What isn't laughable in me cannot be any more so in others, since it's our duty to esteem others more highly than ourselves no matter what, a worldview splendidly in keeping with the earnestness with which I now contemplate the abrupt demise of my sardine pallet. A few of the people near me are conversing as they eat. The earnestness with which they do so is appealing. As long as you're undertaking to do something, you might as well set about it matter-of-factly and with dignity. Dignity and self-confidence have a comforting effect, at least on me they do, and this is why I so like standing around in one of our local Aschingers where people drink, eat, talk, and think all at the same time. How many business ventures were dreamed up here? And best of all: You can remain standing here for hours on end, no one minds, and not one of all the people coming and going will give it a second thought. Anyone who takes pleasure in modesty will get on well here, he can live, no one's stopping him. Anyone who does not insist on particularly heartfelt shows of warmth can still have a heart here, he is allowed that much.

1907

BERLIN W

IT SEEMS that everyone here knows what is proper, and this produces a certain frostiness, and it furthermore seems that everyone here is able to stand his ground from within his own person, and this produces the equanimity that newcomers admire. Poverty appears to have been banished to the districts that border the open fields, or else packed away in the somber, dark interiors of tenements that are blocked from view by the stately residences facing the street as if by massive bodies. It seems as if humanity has stopped heaving sighs here and has begun once and for all to rejoice in its own existence and life. Appearances are deceiving, though: all this elegance and splendor are but a dream. But perhaps the squalor too is only illusory. As for the elegance of Berlin's western districts, it would appear to be characterized by liveliness, though this liveliness is somewhat spoiled because it cannot be cultivated in peace. Everything here, by the way, is caught up in an endless process of cultivation and change. The men are just as modest as they are unchivalrous, and this is something one can feel quite happy about, for chivalry is always three-quarters inappropriate. Gallantry is exceptionally idiotic and impertinent. Accordingly, one seldom witnesses maudlin scenes hereabouts, and when some delicate adventure unfolds, you never even notice, which after all is what constitutes its gentility. Nowadays the world of men is a world of commerce, and a person who is obliged to earn money has little or no time for flamboyantly refined behavior. This explains the brusque tone of voice one often hears. Generally speaking, there is much to be amused by in Berlin West; here you find the most delightfully, sweetly laughable lives you might dream of. Take for example the *dame arriviste*, a feminine force of nature, naïve as a small child. I personally esteem her greatly because she is both so voluptuous and so droll. Or the "little girl from the Kurfürstendamm." She resembles a chamois, and there is much in her that is sweet and good. And here we have the worldly graybeard. Only a very few specimens of this caliber, well versed in savoir vivre, are still sauntering about. The type is dying out, and I find this a tremendous pity. Recently I saw just such a gentleman, and he looked to me like a vision from a vanished age. And here we have something quite different: the rural homesteader who's made good. He hasn't yet divested himself of the habit of gaping as though he were astonished at himself and the good fortune he's plopped down in. He behaves in much too decorous a way, as though he were afraid of revealing his origins. And then we have the very, very severe madam from the age of Bismarck. I am an admirer of severe faces and good manners that have left their mark on the very essence of a person. In general I am moved by age, both in buildings and human beings; by the same token, I find things that are fresh, new, and young no less enlivening; and there's plenty of youthfulness to be found here, and the West does seem to me quite healthy. Must a certain portion of health preclude a certain portion of beauty? By no means! The lively, in the end, is the most beautiful. Well, hmm, perhaps I shall now do a bit of tail-wagging and scraping and flattering; for example with the following sentence: The local women are beautiful and charming! The gardens are tidy, the architecture errs perhaps on the side of the drastic, but what of it? After all, everyone these days is convinced that we are bunglers when it comes to the grandiose, stylish, and monumental, and probably this is because the desire is all too alive within us to possess or produce style, grandeur, and monumentality. Desires are terrible things. Our era is most decidedly an era of sensitivity and righteousness, and this is in fact quite nice on our part. We have public welfare organizations, hospitals, homes for infants, and I like to imagine that this too is worth something. Why should we want everything? Just think of the shivers sent down spines by Fredrick the Great's wars and his—

Sanssouci. We have few contradictions; this demonstrates our longing for a clear conscience. But now I swerve rather badly from my
theme. Is this permitted? There is a so-called Old West Berlin, a
newer West (the area around the Gedächtniskirche), and a very new
West. The middle one is perhaps the nicest. Certainly one finds the
most and greatest elegance on Tauentzienstrasse; the Kurfürstendamm is delightful with its trees and calashes. With great regret I
see that I have now bumped against the frame delimiting my essay,
leaving me with the tragic conviction that many things I most definitely wished to point out have gone unsaid.

1910

TIERGARTEN

STRAINS of regimental music are drifting over from the zoological garden. You stroll along like this, unhurried as you please. Is it not Sunday, after all? How warm it is. Everyone seems astonished to find it suddenly so bright, so clear and warm, as if touched by a magic wand. Warmth alone can give things color. The world in all directions is like a smile, it's enough to put you in a feminine frame of mind. How glad I would be (almost) to be carrying a baby in my arms, playing the role of a devotedly solicitous serving girl. What a tender mood this just-beginning, heart-beguiling spring inspires. I could practically be a mother, or so I imagine. In the spring, it seems, men and manly deeds suddenly become so superfluous, so foolish. No deeds now! Listen, linger, remain rooted to the spot. Be divinely touched by something slight. Gaze into this blissfully sweet, childhood-like green. Ah, Berlin and its Tiergarten are so lovely just now. The park is overrun with people. The people are dark moving spots in the delicate, fleeting sun-shimmer. Up above is the pale-blue sky that touches, dreamlike, the green that lies below. The people walk softly and indolently, as if they feared they might otherwise slip into a marching step and act coarsely. There are said to be people to whom it would never occur—or who might be too prim—to sit on a bench in the Tiergarten on a Sunday. Such people are robbing themselves of the most enchanting pleasure. I myself find the crowd on a Sunday in all its obvious, harmless Sunday pleasure-seeking more significant than any journey to Cairo or the Riviera. Hardness becomes obliging, rigidity dulcet, and all lines, all commonplaces blur dreamily together. A universal strolling like this is ineffably tender. The walkers lose themselves—now one by one, now in grace-ful, tightly knit clusters and groups—among the trees whose high branches are still breezily bare, and between the low bushes that constitute a breath of young, sweet green. The soft air trembles and quivers with buds that seem to sing, to dance, to hover. The image of the Tiergarten as a whole is like a painted picture, then like a dream, then like a circuitous, agreeable kiss. Everywhere one is lightly, com-prehensibly enticed to gaze and linger. On a bench beside the ship-ping canal, two nannies are sitting in their imposing snow-white caps, white aprons, and bright red skirts. Walking, you find yourself satisfied; sitting, you are perfectly calm and gaze with composure into the eyes of the figures walking past. These include children, dogs being led on leashes, soldiers with their girls on their arms, beautiful women, coquettish ladies, men who live, step, and stroll all alone, entire families, bashful lovers. Veils are streaming in the air, green ones, blue ones, and yellow. Dark and light clothing passes in turn. The gentlemen are for the most part wearing those unavoid-able, uninspiring stiff hillock hats of medium height upon their cone-shaped heads. You feel an urge to laugh while remaining sol-emn all the while. Everything is simultaneously droll and sacro-sanct, and this makes you feel solemn like all the others. Everyone is displaying the same appropriate, mild solemnity. Is not the sky do-ing the same with its expression that appears to be saying: "How marvelous I feel"? Now, like friendly specters, wind-like shadows flit through the trees and across the sunlit white paths, and going where? No one knows. You can scarcely see it, that's how delicate it is. Painters draw our attention to such tidbits. At a certain gentle distance, red-wheeled hackney cabs are rolling through the mild green fabric, as though a red ribbon were gliding through a bit of delicate female hair. Everything is emanating womanliness, every-thing is bright and balmy, everything is so wide, so transparent, so round, you turn your Sunday head in all directions to fully relish this Sunday world. It's really the people that comprise it. Without the people, you wouldn't see, notice, or experience the beauty of the Tiergarten. What's the crowd like here? Well, it's a mixed bag, all sorts of people tumbled in together, the elegant and the simple, the proud and the humble, the gay and the grim. I myself, by my very presence, add to the colorfulness of the scene and contribute to the mix. I'm certainly enough of a mixture myself. But where is the dream? Do let's take one more look at it. Upon a roundly arched bridge many people are standing. You stand there yourself, leaning lightly and in the best of spirits against the railing to gaze down into the delicately blue, glimmering warm water where boats and skiffs, filled with people and adorned with little flags, drift quietly about as if drawn on by good premonitions. The ships and gondolas shimmer in the sunlight. Now a piece of dark velvet-green breaks from the brightness, it is a blouse. Ducks with colorful heads are swaying upon the ripples and quiverings of water that sometimes shimmers like bronze or enamel. How splendid it is the way the field of the water is so narrow and circumscribed and yet so packed with gliding pleasure boats and hats in all the colors of joy. Everywhere you look, a lady's hat gleams and bursts from the bushes with red and blue and other pleasures for the eye. How simple it all is. And where should one go now? To a coffeehouse? Really? Can one really be so barbaric? Indeed, one can. Such things a person does! How lovely to be doing something that another person is doing as well. And how lovely the Tiergarten is. What resident of Berlin could fail to adore it?

1911

IN THE ELECTRIC TRAM

RIDING the "electric" is an inexpensive pleasure. When the car arrives, you climb aboard, possibly after first politely ceding the right of way to an imposing gentlewoman, and then the car continues on. At once you notice that you have a rather musical disposition. The most delicate melodies are parading through your head. In no time you've elevated yourself to the position of a leading conductor or even composer. Yes, it's really true: the human brain involuntarily starts composing songs in the electric tram, songs that in their involuntary nature and their rhythmic regularity are so very striking that it's hard to resist thinking oneself a second Mozart.

Meanwhile you have rolled yourself a cigarette, say, and inserted it with great care between your well-practiced lips. With such an apparatus in your mouth, it is impossible to feel utterly without cheer, even if your soul happens to be torn in twain by sufferings. But is this the case? Most certainly not. Just wanted to give a quick description of the magic that a smoking white object of this sort is capable of working, year in and year out, on the human psyche. And what next?

Our car is constantly in motion. It is raining in the streets we glide through, and this constitutes one more added pleasantness. Some people find it frightfully agreeable to see that it is raining and at the same time be permitted to sense that they themselves are not getting wet. The image produced by a gray, wet street has something consoling and dreamy about it, and so you stand now upon the rear platform of the creaking car that is rumbling its way forward, and you gaze straight ahead. Gazing straight ahead is something done by almost all the people who sit or stand in the "electric."

People do, after all, tend to get somewhat bored on such trips, which often require twenty or thirty minutes or even more, and what do you do to provide yourself with some modicum of entertainment? You look straight ahead. To show by one's gaze and gestures that one is finding things a bit tedious fills a person with a quite peculiar pleasure. Now you return to studying the face of the conductor on duty, and now you content yourself once more with merely, vacantly staring straight ahead. Isn't that nice? One thing and then another? I must confess: I have achieved a certain technical mastery in the art of staring straight ahead.

It is prohibited for the conductor to converse with the esteemed passengers. But what if prohibitions are sidestepped, laws violated, admonitions of so refined and humane a nature disregarded? This happens fairly often. Chatting with the conductor offers prospects of the most charming recreation, and I am particularly adept at seizing opportunities to engage in the most amusing and profitable conversations with this tramway employee. It pays to ignore certain regulations, and summoning one's powers to render uniforms loquacious helps create a convivial mood.

From time to time you do nonetheless look straight ahead again. After completing this straightforward exercise, you may permit your eyes a modest excursion. Your gaze sweeps through the interior of the car, crossing fat, drooping mustaches, the face of a weary, elderly woman, a pair of youthfully mischievous eyes belonging to a girl, until you've had your fill of these studies in the quotidian and gradually begin to observe your own footgear, which could use proper mending. And always new stations are arriving, new streets, and the journey takes you past squares and bridges, past the war ministry and the department store, and all this while it is continuing to rain, and you continue to behave as if you were a tad bored, and you continue to find this conduct the most suitable.

But it might also be that while you were riding along like that, you heard or saw something beautiful, gay, or sad, something you will never forget.

1908

THE METROPOLITAN STREET

SOME OF the streets in the historic city center appear strangely deserted; a cathedral in its venerable glory, monotonous barracks, and an old castle serve only to heighten the sense of stillness and isolation. In the dimly lit, stolidly middle-class beer halls, a few evening guests sit at the tables reading newspapers; the waiter stands idle, a napkin clamped beneath his arm. In another district a few streets away, people are hurrying along shoulder to shoulder and at each other's heels; no one is chasing them, but, as it appears, no one is beckoning them either. These hundred hurriers have similar destinations and are coming from places that very much resemble one another, and all of them maintain a measured gravity admirable in its way. The trees are strangely green, not like in other cities. A silent cemetery from olden days borders one of the busiest streets upon whose bumpy pavement hackney cabs, horse-drawn carts, and omnibuses ceaselessly roll. In various Aschinger branches, beer is ceaselessly poured into glasses, and all these glasses being filled one after the other find takers and drinkers. The managers of these places of entertainment comport themselves like officers on the field of battle, and officers are seen going about their business, silent, staid, sedate, and modest, as though they've tired of putting on a show of valor, as is surely the case for some of them. When you cross from one sidewalk to the other, you must take care not to get run over, but this caretaking goes unnoticed, it has become a habit. How this great city both hinders and feeds on the movements of human beings. People who live in its northern districts have gone perhaps a full year now without setting eyes on the bright, elegant districts to the west, and it's difficult to see what might prompt a lady residing in a western district to visit the neighborhood surrounding Schlesischer Bahnhof in the east unless she had some quite particular cause.

You rarely see the frail and infirm hereabouts, and this is no doubt above all because invalids and the weary have every reason to avoid this constant stream of traffic and instead keep to the quiet of home. The people you find circulating on the street are more or less hardy and energetic, and display a gay-hearted vivacity, if only because they sense that propriety requires this, and because all who live and walk here rise to the occasion with a certain unobtrusive courtesy. Sulky or despondent persons are forced to dampen their sulkiness and despondency if only out of purely practical considerations; hotheads are compelled to cool their heads; an individual tempted to laugh aloud for sheer delight instantly comprehends that this is not allowed; and one whose eyes well up with tears quickly turns to gaze into a shop window as if oh so fascinated by what he sees there. The flirt avails himself of the simplest and at the same time subtlest measures. Although you might have the impression that strangers shy away from one another in the streets and squares and trams, assiduously avoiding every contact or emotion, a great many lovely, sweet exchanges do nonetheless occur, more than the observer might suspect or the nonlocal manage to observe, precisely because the one undertaking or planning something acts as though he were just aimlessly daydreaming or pondering. Should some minor unpleasantness occur—be it that a horse loses its footing on ground often smooth as glass and falls, be it that a brawl or something of the sort erupts—a generally attractive clutch of onlookers immediately gathers about the novelty, responding neither with indifference nor with any sort of vehemence to the interruption.

Everything is clean. Shop windows gleam with the same meticulous cleanliness as the utterances of the people, the schooled and unschooled alike; the maidservant takes on the bearing of her employer, and the lady of the house leaves all dignity and aloofness behind when she exits the door of her home. The droll, innocent schoolboy brings his report card home on the very same "electric" that is also transporting the harlot or a person who is using this time to hatch criminal plans, and not one of them bristles at the others' presence. Many eyes shine with secret longing, many lips are pressed tightly together, many souls are trembling, but everything wishes to be seemly and correct, to take its logical course; everything can and will preserve itself. The streets resemble one another just as human destinies do, and yet every street has its own character, and you can never compare one destiny to another. As for elegance, one generally seeks and understands it best by choosing not to cultivate it; the greatest charm of elegance lies in a certain negligence, approximately like the noblesse of thought and feeling that is lost the moment it begins to struggle for expression, or like style in language, which fails when it tries to come to the fore.

In the greatness and pride of this city lies a certain unmistakable stillness; and all its sounds are crowned with a soundlessness so powerful that when a person has spent some time in rural silence and retirement, he longs to hear it once more to refresh his soul. And it is clear beyond all doubt that in the metropolis a pronounced need to avoid all superfluous rushing and haste predominates. Eating and drinking well count for a great deal here; the hungry feel anger toward their fellow men and therefore are always running up against others everywhere they go, be it with a sharp elbow or the scowls on their aggrieved, disgruntled faces. Disgruntlement is an enemy of mankind and also of the pointlessly languishing disgruntled person himself, and because it is impossible to avoid this feeling when many people find themselves pressed together in close proximity, one might say that every city, once it grows into a metropolis, gradually rids itself of this or that percentage of the annoyance that fruitlessly grieves and groans out its days there, as grudging grievers generally cannot stomach the company of others. Oh, certainly! Often we are filled with anger, fury, or hatred, but then we go and dilute ourselves, in other words seek out human company, and behold: the ills afflicting our souls quickly vanish. A sort of noble, far-seeing socialism is gaining ground here in a quite natural way, and class hatred appears no longer to exist outside the newspapers that paint its portrait. Every lowly worker or day laborer who excels in mental and physical health can calmly triumph, noting the appearance of wealthy folk who suffer physical complaints, a circumstance they are often unable to conceal; and so it is the sickly, not the poor who must be pitied, and the disenfranchised are the ones in poor health, not those who happen to have lowly origins. The metropolitan street teaches us this lesson quite convincingly. Oh Lord, enough for now, I have to go out, have to leap down into the world, I can't stand it any longer, I have got to go laugh in someone's face, I must go for a walk. Ah, how lovely, how very lovely it is to be alive.

1910

THE THEATER

THE THEATER, A DREAM

THE THEATER is a like a dream. In the Greek theater, things might have been different; ours is mysteriously, exotically enclosed in a roof-covered, dark building. You go inside, and then a few hours later you emerge again as if from a peculiar slumber, returning to nature and to real life, and the dream is dispelled.

In this dream, the images rising up before the eye—which might be the soul's eye—have something sharp and firmly sketched about them. Natural spatial perspectives, actual ground beneath one's feet, and fresh air do not exist here. You inhale bedroom air while striding across mountains like the man with Seven League Boots. In this dream, everything is reduced in scale but also becomes more fearsome; faces generally bear unsettlingly fixed expressions: terribly sweet when the face is sweet and benevolent, and terribly repulsive when it's a horror- and fear-inspiring one. In dreams we experience the ideal dramatic foreshortening. A dream's voices possess a bewitching pliancy, its language is eloquent and at the same time well-considered; its images show us the magic of the enchanting and unforgettable because they are hyperreal, simultaneously genuine and unnatural. The hues of these images are at once sharp and soft, they cut into the eye with their sharpness like whetted knives slicing into an apple, and then are gone the next moment, so that you often—even while still in the midst of your dream—feel sorry to see certain things vanish so swiftly.

Our theater is like a dream, and it has every reason to become even more like one. In Germany everything wants to be enveloped and enclosed, everything wants to have a roof. Even the poor, pompous works of sculpture in our gardens are dreams—but for the most part these dreams are frozen. It's a well-known fact how bad we are at public monuments. Amid the wafting breezes of freedom, we find ourselves devoid of talent. We'd rather step into a dear, dreamlike, strange building where we encounter our true breezes, our true nature. Why are we so skilled at hosting Christmas festivities, why are we happy to sit in a warm room and watch as it snows, gusts, blusters, or rains outdoors? We so like to spend time in dark, introspective holes. This penchant is not itself a weakness; our weakness is that we feel ashamed of it.

Are not works of literature also dreams, and is the open stage anything other than their wide-open mouth speaking as if in sleep? During the taxing day, we drive our business interests and useful intentions before us through the streets and various establishments, and then we assemble in these narrow rows of seats, like narrow beds, to gaze and hear; the curtain—the lip of this mouth—springs open, and we find ourselves being disconcertingly yet also intimately addressed, roaringly, hissingly, with flickering tongues and smiles, which fills us with a frenzy we wouldn't wish to subdue, nor would we be able to; it makes us writhe with laughter or else tremble with heartfelt tears. The images blaze and burn before our eyes, the figures in the play move before us like unnaturally large, unfamiliar apparitions. The bedroom is dark, only the open dream is resplendent in the bright lights—dazzling, speaking—and we are compelled to sit there with open mouths.

How melodious are the colors in a dream! They seem to be turning into faces, and suddenly a color threatens, sobs, sings, or smiles; a river becomes a horse, and the horse is about to climb a narrow staircase with its hoofed feet; the knight is forcing it, he is being pursued, they intend to tear his heart from his body, they are getting closer, in the distance you can see the murderers racing toward him, a nameless fear seizes you—the curtain falls. An earthquake strikes a municipal square, the buildings sink and tilt, the air appears to be splattered with blood, fiery-red wounds are hanging everywhere; people are firing their rifles, meaning to compete with nature in murderousness; all the while the sky is a sweet pale blue, but it lies so childishly above the buildings, like a painted sky. This bleeding is like small roses being thrown about; the buildings keep falling and yet they stand, and constantly there is a horrific screaming and the crack of rifle fire and yet there is none. Oh, how divinely this dream is playacting! It presents incontestably pure images of the horrific, but also of sweetness, oppression, melancholy, and anxious remembrance. It instantly paints settings to match sentiments, persons, and sounds, supplementing the sweet prattling of a virtuous woman with her face, giving snakes the strange weeds from which they horrifically slither forth; the cries of the drowning the dreary evening landscape of river and shore; and a smile the mouth that expresses it.

Amid dark-green bushes, white faces lean out, each with a request, a plaint or with hatred in its horrifically clear eyes. Sometimes we see only features, lines, sometimes only eyes; then the pale features come and frame these eyes, then come the wild black waves of hair and bury the face; then once more there is only a voice, then a door opens; two figures charge in, you try to wake up, but the inexorable charging-in continues. There are moments in a dream whose memory stays with us as long as we live.

This is the effect of the theater too with its figures, words, notes, sounds, and colors. Who would wish to see a delightful love scene minus the opulently overgrown garden in which it occurs, a murder without the dark wall of the alleyway, a scream without the window through which it rings out, the window without the delicate and feminine white curtain that makes it a window, lending it magic and yet also naturalism? Snowy landscapes, nocturnal ones, lie upon the stage in such a way as to make one believe they extend and stretch for miles; a train with red-shimmering windows passes by, quite slowly, as though it were wending and winding its way far off into the distance, where the swift does not insist on receding swiftly from the eye. The distant and the near lie side by side in the theater. Two scoundrels are always whispering too loudly; the noble gentleman hears it all, and yet he pretends utter ignorance. This is what is so dreamlike, so truly untrue, so poignant, and in the end so beautiful.

How beautiful it is when two men whisper to each other at the top of their lungs while the expression of the other one says to us: how quiet it is all around me!

Such things are like the gruesome and beautiful stories in dreams. The stage does its utmost to terrify; it does well to have such aims, and we do well to foster that something within us that allows us to be receptive to the pleasure and frisson this terror brings.

1907

A PERSON POSSESSED OF CURIOSITY

WHAT PLAYS will be put on this winter, what protagonists will walk the stage, what manner of authors will be heard from, and with the help of what sorts of wires will performances be launched in all the theaters of the capital? That is the—once again, as it appears to me—not entirely uncrucial question. Probably there will be a play by Hauptmann, one by Sudermann, and one by Wedekind, and apropos one by Hofmannsthal, and I must confess that it didn't cost me much mental exertion to be compelled to trumpet out all of this. But will there also be some new name emerging from the vast shadows of as-yet-unknownness, will novelties be served up? Let me venture to assume so and to believe that we shall have sparks rained down upon us by luminaries in the southeast. What will Reinhardt be putting on? Will he have some good trumps to play, and what are our best-known critics currently up to? Are they still sitting at the edge of the woods reading books or smoking pipes? Soon they will have to come flitting this way at a proper clip, for things here are about to heat up, and we shall have heartfelt need of this cooling fire brigade. What are the actors doing? Where are their not yet burnt-out Vesuviuses of creative verve to be found? Be careful there with your sunshiny high spirits and flames of enthusiasm! People are already standing here in formation with their pointy water hoses—i.e., pens—behind their ears, ready to give you a good squirting should you overestimate your own achievement. Where is youth, and where are the undiscovered talents, and where, if this query meets with approval, are the esteemed high- and lowborn dramaturges currently traveling? I believe I see one of them strolling up and down the lively streets of Copenhagen on the arm of a pretty wench. They should watch out or someone might take them down a notch. Soon this luxuriant summer world will, thank God, have come to an end, and what I meant to ask was: When is the first important premiere, on what day will it take place, and will it be thrilling? I do hope so, for I am of the sort who lick their lips at the prospect of premiere night, which they quite possibly expect to be a banquet. Not that I'd say I enjoy it when a playwright is hissed and decried, but I do enjoy it all the same, as there is always some enjoyment to be found in the lamentable.

When will the curtain rise for the first time to allow us to gaze down upon uplifting scenes? Will there be much that uplifts? I'd like to hope there will also be, now and again, something degrading to be seen, something shameless, so to speak, since it must after all be reckoned among the secret pleasures of a theatergoer to be permitted to find sufficient grounds to blush. Things should prick and prickle a bit, otherwise it might get dull, and after all, there are always people who enjoy this, as well as some who are swiftly inclined to find everything tedious. Did the stage-set painters give their brushes a proper cleaning during the vacation? Is there oil in the lamps? Are there innovations with regard to the lighting? But this is perhaps significantly less important than the breathless question of how things stand with the actors' gestures. It's to be hoped that one or the other of the individuals in question has smoothed his rough edges a little, and as for the noble dexterity of tongue, we are expecting miracles this year:

> I wish the night would swallow me. Again
> I have been wandering in the moonlight unawares.

Have the daggers been polished, buttons shined, stones hewn, benches cobbled together, curtains painted, moldings gilded, shirts pressed, manners scrubbed, heads washed, bodies steeled; are the senses fresh, the shoes free of holes, and all hearts in good fettle? Let's assume so. How will the gentlemen make their entrances? Clad in armor or suit jackets? And the ladies? Will they wear velvet gowns or else dress-reform garments? In the end it's a matter of complete indifference how they stand out, provided they know how to make a grand entrance—for this, I believe when I gaze innovatively into space as I am doing at this moment, is all that truly matters.

> I crept into the garden here exhausted
> And when the night enfolded me so sweetly—

Lovely, isn't it?

1907

ON THE RUSSIAN BALLET

HOW RAVISHING, the Russian ballerinas from the Imperial Theatre in Petersburg. They dance very well, and now in Berlin they have garnered much acclaim and are enjoying great success that they are generally felt to deserve. Perhaps this is revealing, perhaps not, but in any case we were very satisfied, very pleased, and for the most part even enchanted. A few of the dancers dazzled us. Among these Russians there is one great artist, Anna Pavlova, a very conscious, very intelligent, and up to certain limits doubtless also brilliant artist. Local papers have dubbed her the queen of dance, and apparently that's what she is. She's just marvelous. Ah, this Berlin with its love and understanding of the arts, how peculiar it is in so many respects! And then success itself—how odd it often is! But enough of this. Let us speak of dulcet, dancerly things, and not of such foolish ones, such—I almost want to say—thickheaded, clumsy matters as success and its manufacture. Let us be merry, rich, light, earnest, courteous, virtuous, and well-mannered.

There's no doubt a touch of parvenu effrontery in this desire on the part of someone of my ilk, who has never studied dance, to engage in scribbling and scrabbling on the theme, topic, and subject of dancing. And yet my sympathies are so vibrant that I cannot possibly bring myself to say: "No, I shall not write." And what harm does it do, when one's breast is filled with pleasurable sentiments, to make a bit of a fool of oneself? Yes, pleasurable sentiments, ravishing faces, lovely, beautiful gestures, dulcet memories, reasons for gratitude and veneration have all been bequeathed to us as a gift by the Russian ballet. There's one perfectly ridiculous piece: *Harlequin's Millions*.

Anna Pavlova sits like a youthful regent upon a rickety, implausible, small balcony, gazing with wonderful gestures upon the crowd below—Italians apparently—who apparently are indulging in all manner of nocturnal, adventuresome, serenading, troubadourish pastimes. And perhaps daintiest, most dazzling, and loveliest of all was this magic spell of a balcony.

Clearly the play's burden is the triumph of tender love over greed and the attempts of old age to act foolish and young. Or something of the sort. *Item*, we then see this balcony splendor glide to the ground, and now she begins to dance sweetness and greatness. "Now that is dance," a highly enthused person said to me during intermission. "No doubt," I replied, and this dissembling dryness pleased me. "Stupendous," a second person said. I couldn't help laughing. Oh, this Berlin when its enthusiasms are aroused. Naturally I am of the deeply felt conviction that it is quite nice, quite lovely to be capable of enthusiasm. Novelty enthuses. And these Russian dancers and danseuses struck us as utterly novel and unprecedented. Their traditional dances appeared bold, unique, and new. We were dazzled by an art that the mature and intelligent among us had believed dead and buried.

Is this ballet the future? For a dance to live on beyond the one tumultuous success, pieces must be written that correspond to our time and its spirit. As for the rest, it isn't at all necessary to understand the art of dance. We don't have to know what a certain delightful movement of the hand and arm signifies. All we have to do is feel it and see it, and for this reason thinking about the future of this dance that's been passed down to us is rather philistine. But often it's not a bad idea to practice a bit of philistinism.

Utterly marvelous and downright uplifting are the solo dances performed by these people from the realm of czars, the national and folk dances. Even just the costumes themselves. And then this beautiful wildness ennobled by discipline and tact. It's enchanting, and here the dancer Eduardova must be mentioned. She represents sensual beauty, while Pavolva stands for spiritual enchantment.

It was clearly apparent that this tremendously, prodigiously modern Berlin no longer possesses a ballet audience. A ballet is the sort of spectacle that ought to be enjoyed coolheadedly or at any rate with a great deal of gentlemanly and gentlewomanly sophistication: fleetingly, poshly, coldly, elegantly, and solemnly—in the midnight hour, for example, between clever repartee and a rousing bottle of wine. After all, it's not an Ibsen play, not a Wagnerian opera being performed. And since here in Berlin it's been a long, long time since we've experienced "something of the sort"—in other words, since we are no longer used to seeing a ballet as something purely and delightfully pleasurable—we've been thinking of it as somehow anxiety-provoking and thus, I believe myself justified in saying, as almost too, too significant. Well, one ought not speak so philistinely. But it was profound to see how it enflamed us to witness this display of grace. Have we been thirsting for grace? It would seem so.

Beauty has caught us off our guard once more. A real ambush. And the detractors attended so as to blissfully, besottedly worship the objects of decades of surfeit. This is a sign of the age we live in: extreme wavering—in any case with regard to what is known as bon ton, our understanding of art, and taste. It all sends us whirling, and so we whirl! That we are still capable of feeling joy and the most heartfelt delight, and feeling them without warning, should give us a certain satisfaction. What blusterers we are! But perhaps this is necessary. And this too should be stated: We owe thanks to the people who had the idea of inviting these talented Russian dancers to try their luck once more in the capital of the Reich. After all, last year we virtually snubbed the noble Pavlova along with the rest of her band of artistes, or in any case heaped on them the frost of half-hearted accolades.

I thought it would be fitting to try to underscore all these things. Relating how beautifully she danced, this great artist Anna Pavlova, is beyond me. She inspires the poet to write poems, the painter to sketch out paintings, the musician to envision new musical works. She is at once delicate and audacious, grand and humble, beautiful and significant. Ah, her smile, and her magnificent sweeping stride. Her miraculous arms and legs. Just look at the balcony. There she sits, gesturing in a way that would befit a fairy-tale queen, toward all these eyes and hearts filled with loving admiration. Does she not resemble a seductive enchantress casting a spell that makes it appear to us that sweetness and nobility can never entirely die out in this world?

1909

PORTRAIT SKETCH

It's as if I saw him before me, the Prince of Homburg. He's had period costume slapped on him and now appears to be piquing himself on the colors of this garb, that's how vain a fellow he is. He's also quite a talent, incidentally: he speaks well, and this gives him one more thing to pique himself on. He has tall, gleamingly polished boots on his firmly planted legs, and, good heavens, chivalric gloves on his hands, which not everyone has; a mere bourgeois, for example, would not be wearing any such thing. Upon his head sits a wig, and his mustache is fabulously curly—this alone being enough to ensure artistic success. All he has to do now is stamp his soldierly leg on the ground in vexation to sweep away all malevolent critiques; he does so, and from this moment on this Monsieur Prince of Homburg is a divinely gifted artist. Moreover, he's learned his lines by heart, which is utterly superfluous, and has made a note of the passages where his entire princely Homburgly nature is to shine through—an absolute lack of artistic unselfconsciousness. He doesn't have to be able to do anything, in fact it's even good if he can't, as a true actor opposes learning—his abilities are inborn. After all, that's what laudably separates this lofty profession from all other earthly professions: one simply stomps to the fore in one's boots, rattles one's dagger about, gesticulates, and reaps applause. It isn't an ordinary person who can succeed in saying:

Balanced upon your sphere, oh most vast Fortune—

Such words cannot be spoken by a doctor, mechanic, journalist, bookbinder, or mountain climber, nor would such a person, as God is my witness, have any reason to utter them. The eyes of the Prince of Homburg roll frightfully within their sockets, he speaks these lines more with his rolling eyes than with his lips. He speaks these lines badly, by the way, which demonstrates that he is a good person, that he has a soul, a wife and child, that he has character, and it demonstrates as well—yes, this has only now struck me—that he has thought very, very deeply about his role. This Prince of Homburg displays an enchanting Arcadianism when the time comes for him to say:

> Pah!—As a rogue would write it, not a prince.—
> I'll find some other turn of phrase.

He might possibly bellow these words. And now he expects applause, but he feels himself to be aristocratically exalted above the burgher whose applause he desires. Well, after all, he is an aristocrat, a landowner with property along the Rhine:

> And there I'll work at building and tearing down.

My goodness, he really does lose himself in the part he is playing. Talent is something possessed by the cobbler who measured him for those high-shafted boots, not by him, or in other words: Why, of course he has talent, but what does any of this mean to a burgher of simple birth?

1907

ON STAGING LIES

WE ARE living now in a peculiar time, though all times may perhaps have had their own timely peculiarities. Indeed, this time of ours strikes me as highly, highly peculiar, especially when—as I am doing just now—I place one finger alongside my nose so as to reflect upon the actual nature of this life that we are now forcefully thrusting and squeezing onto the stage. We give the stage life to eat, and it appears to be well fed. Even the most obscure, sequestered dramatist presents the theater with his scraps of obscure, sequestered life. If things continue at such a clip, life will soon be lying flat on its back like a consumption-wracked crone, sucked and pumped dry to the ribs, while the theater will be as plump, portly, and stuffed full as, say, an engineer who's struck gold with his patented enterprises and is now in a position to allow himself all the pleasures the world affords.

The stage needs life! True enough, but plague and pox confound it, where is all this good, wholesome, veritable life supposed to come from? From life, no? But then is life really so inexhaustible? In my view it is inexhaustible only insofar as we let it keep on following its natural course—tranquil, fluid, and broad—like an untamed, beautiful river. But it may soon appear incontrovertible that we erudite numskulls are merely exploiting and pummeling life, no longer its natural children. It's as if life were a large, dusty carpet that now, in this age of ours, is to be hung out and given a good whacking. Even dentists who've gone to see *Lulu* have begun to study the features and muscles of life as though it were necessary to cut open an old cadaver and hurl pieces of it onto the stage.

Here's the thing: the more vivid and natural things look at the theater, the more anxious, guarded, vexed, and upholstered things will appear in everyday life. When the stage bangs out its truths, it exerts an intimidating influence; when, however, it spins out golden, idealized falsehoods in an oversize, unnaturally beautiful form—as it used to do at least a little in former eras—the effect of this is provocative and heartening, it fosters the beautiful, crass vulgarities of life. Then we can say we've been to the theater and luxuriated in a foreign, noble, beautiful, gentle world. Watch out with those unbridled nature plays of yours, lest life trickle away unawares. I'm all for a theater of lies, Lord help me.

1907

DO YOU KNOW MEIER?

MEIER spelled with an "ei"? No? Well, in that case I should like to permit myself to humbly draw your attention to this man. He is currently appearing at Café Bümplitz, which is situated on some street I can no longer recall. There, amid bad and unseemly tobacco fumes, rude remarks, and the clatter of tankard lids, he performs night after night and will go on doing so until one day perhaps some clever theater management will scoop him up, which I don't doubt for a moment will shortly occur. This man, this Meier, this fellow is a genius. It's not just that he can make you laugh harder than twenty men can laugh in all their added-together lives, make you laugh till you split your sides or, what am I saying, till you roll in the aisles, or wait a bit, till you die laughing, oh what a simpleton I am if I cannot pound a better comparison from the quarry of my authorial cranium, it's not just that but also that, how confusing this is, yes, quite right, but also that even the quite natural inducement of a tragic frisson is by no means beyond his reach, in fact he finds it all too easy. So have I actually finished my sentence now or not? If not, what a lovely pretext for going on.

Meier also performs music-hall ditties with a fabulous don't-mind-if-I-do-ishness, speaking a language that is surely the most unimpeachable there is, for he lets it drop, nugget by nugget as it were, such that a person listening to him might take a notion to kneel at the man's feet to gather up the morsels. The tone of this voice—I've studied it in considerable depth—reproduces in sound the approximate impression made on the eye by the progress of a snail, so resplendently languorous, so lazy, so brown, so very reptant, so slimy, so gluey, and so terribly if-not-today-why-not-tomorrow. A pleasure pure and simple. I can recommend it in good conscience.

This Meier, one should know if one does not know it already, plays a theater usher, the role he most shines in, a figure with horrifying trousers, a tall hat, a stuck-on nose, a box beneath his arm, holes at his elbows, cigar in mouth, and not just a lip on him but a proper maw, and a bundle of bad jokes on his dunderhead tongue. This figure is beyond delightful. I for my part have seen him, just a sec, I think a good fifty times now and still have not tired of the act. Of course not! One never tires of gazing upon excellence.

A small stage, harsh lighting, upon the stage a table and beside it a chair—this is to represent the office of a management director. The manager herself, a slender, youthful female, announces that she now has everything she needs to launch a cycle of performances, the only thing still lacking is an usher, this is a problem, but she has already had advertisements placed in the newspapers and is eager to see who will respond.

And who should enter now like a wraith from the underworld? Meier! Why of course, devil take it, what else was to be expected, but look, the wonderful part is that you nonetheless find yourself utterly astounded by the novelty with which this Meier spelled with an "ei" is capable of trouser-legging his way up the stairs, in a manner that leaves you no choice but to think he must have done something it would be improper to say aloud in good company.

He reports to the horrified lady, who surely has read Oscar Wilde, with a circumlocutoriness that would be unsuitable on any other lips, he asks and does the most foolish things, then asks yet other things, is about to take his leave, then enters once more, leaves again, but only in order to appear all over again, always with greater impudence, always more indecorous in his demeanor, speech, manner, gestures, tone, and bearing. And all the while he displays the most astonishing talent for uttering some well-timed bit of filth, and uttering it how? *How* is something you have to have heard with your own ears. Evening after evening, a good twenty or thirty patrons, on Saturdays and Sundays eighty, one hundred, or one hundred and fifteen, or even one more than that come to hear him.

I've already pointed out that Meier can also make a tragic impression. In order to achieve this, he quite simply changes his voice and throws his hands in the air, a strategy that until now has always worked. Then he becomes a madman, a King Leer—not Lear but Leer, because during this production he looks at the audience in such a way that all present do exactly what is described in the line: And in haste betook them home. I alone am in the habit of remaining. And then I experience what it means to feel terror when suddenly the voice of a human being becomes a towering edifice, as is the case with Meier's, an edifice at whose open windows and doors some unknown monstrosity is bellowing. How I shake with fear on each and every occasion, and how glad I am when this Meier with all his terrifying "oho"s and "ha"s and "hey"s once more becomes simply a Meier with an "ei."

1907

FOUR AMUSEMENTS

1.

ON THE top floor at Wertheim's, where people have coffee, something delectable is currently on view: the dramatic poet Seltmann. Perched atop a small cane stool upon an elevated pedestal, an easy target for passing glances, he ceaselessly hammers, nails, pounds, and cobbles together—as it appears to all observing him—lines of blank verse. The small, rectangular pedestal is tastefully wreathed with dark-green fir twigs. The poet is clad respectably: tailcoat, patent-leather shoes, and white cravat are all represented, and no one need feel embarrassed to give this man his full attention. What's marvelous, though, is the splendid shock of russet hair arching from Seltmann's head past his shoulders and plummeting to the floor. It resembles the mane of a lion. Who is this Seltmann? Will he liberate us from the ignominy of seeing our theater in the hands of so many saltpeter factories? Will he write our national drama? Will he someday appear to be the one we've been pining for so black-puddingishly? In any case we must be grateful to the directors of the Wertheim department store for putting Seltmann on display.

2.

That the theater is gradually losing its best and most sterling capacities can, to our great chagrin, be gathered from a letter that celebrated actress Gertrud Eysoldt has addressed to us. She informs us that she will soon be opening a corset shop on Kantstrasse at the corner of Joachimstaler Strasse, where she will establish herself exclusively as a businesswoman. What an odd resolve, and how regrettable! The actor Kayssler also intends to abscond, and this for the reason that, as we hear, he feels that under the prevailing temporalities it is more appropriate to stand behind the bar in a pub than portray figurines upon the stage. He's said to have taken over a little bar in one of the city's eastern districts that will be opening on May first, and is already looking forward, as several people report, to dispensing beer, washing glasses, preparing sandwiches, serving up kippers, and boot-blacking drunken louts out the door in the wee hours. A crying shame. We, however, deeply regret seeing two so highly admired and esteemed artists betraying their art in such fashion. Let us hope that such conduct does not become a trend.

3.

At the Kammerspiele a minor change was instituted at the eleventh hour. The management dressed up the dramaturgical staff in handsome light-blue tailcoats complete with large silver buttons. We declare this attractive, for it strikes us as appropriate. The ushers have been abolished, and the dramaturges—who after all have nothing else to do on performance nights—take the ladies' coats and show the theater's patrons to their seats. They also open doors and dispense all sorts of trifling but crucial bits of information. On their legs they now wear long, thick, buff-colored, knee-high gaiters, and they are already quite adept at handing out programs with an elegant bow and offering opera glasses. In the provinces they would also distribute leaflets, but here in Berlin this is unnecessary. In short, no critic shall ever again have cause to wonder what a dramaturge is and what sorts of duties he fulfills. They are now exerting themselves to the utmost, and in future one will have no choice but to leave them in peace.

4.

Wishing to rid himself once and for all of the eternal grumbling and the constant reproach that he only ever stages sets rather than plays, director Reinhardt has hit on the idea of, in future, simply having his plays take place before a backdrop of white linens. Naturally his dramaturges couldn't resist letting the cat out of the bag, and he will be astonished if not indignant to see us trumpeting forth this news today already. White linens! Well, do they have to be snow-white? Could they not be worn, say, for a day and a half by some unknown lady giant from the sideshow? Then the various bits of the set would exude an assuredly ravishing fragrance of thighs that could only do the critics good, as it would cause them to forget where they were sitting and beguile all their sharpest senses. Seriously. Reinhardt's idea strikes us as quite promising, in other words brilliant. Against the white cloth, the faces and ghostly figures of the actors and actresses will make a strikingly colorful impression. But will Reinhardt also succeed in gaining acceptance for this notion at the Hoftheater?

1907

COWSHED

I WENT to see Bonn. I beheld him in his famous checked Sherlock Holmes suit. The sight of his tawny leather spats devastated me. But it is far from my intention to make so bold as to speak of Bonn, whom I also learned to admire as Edmund Kean in the play by Dumas. Today, with the kind reader's permission, I wish to speak of the Cowshed, an artistic singsong and jinglejangle establishment that lies in the northern reaches of our beloved city, Berlin. At the Cowshed, among other things, I met and learned to revere beyond all measure a Swiss girl who figured as a waitress there. There are figures galore at the Cowshed. I myself am a not unpopular, at times even celebrated regular. When I set foot on the premises, which are redolent of an aging, half-dead elegance, the publican gets up from his seat where he is keeping watch and greets me with great amicability by making a thoroughly courteous, suave bow, the significance of which is that I should buy a round of cognac. Oh, the conduct I display here at the Cowshed. It resembles the conduct of a Prince Dolgoroucki, a Count Osten-Sacken, a Prince Poniatowski. I always treat the artistes assembled upon the small triangular stage, which is stuck in a corner as if lost in indeterminacy and incertitude, to a boot. The significance of the term "boot" in localities such as the Cowshed is no doubt unfamiliar to most ladies and gentlemen of a literary bent. A boot of this sort is quite simply a tankard of beer shaped like a lady's boot, made of glass and holding nearly two liters. The music made at the Cowshed is often ear-rending; nonetheless I do adore it and dream of divinely beautiful things whenever it creeps into my ear to ensnare me with melodies. Invariably I have some refreshment placed upon the fortepiano of the bushy-haired, gasconading lout of a band leader. This amenity, which he loses no time in appreciating and, as for the rest, most artfully guzzling, ah pardon, I mean drinking, consists in nothing other than various glasses of beer. Yes, I do have to say that quite a lot of money exits my pockets at the Cowshed. Excellent interest accrues on the capital thus invested, and this interest takes the form of merriments that give me no end of pleasure. For the most part I am a most cleverly respectable fellow, but at times, at times . . . when the mood happens to strike . . .

1911 (?)

AN ACTOR

THE ABYSSINIAN lion at the Zoological Garden is most interesting. He's performing in a tragedy, one that shows him simultaneously languishing and growing fat. He despairs (a nameless despair) and at the same time keeps himself nice and round. He thrives and at the same time is slowly tormenting himself to death. And all of this plays out before the eyes of the assembled spectators. I myself stood for a long time before his cage, utterly incapable of tearing my eyes away from this kingly drama. On a side note, incidentally: I should like to change professions, if this might be done expeditiously and with little effort, and become a painter of animals. I'd be able to paint my fill just of this caged-in lion. Has the esteemed literary reader ever looked closely and with proper attentiveness at the eye of an elephant? It sparkles with primordial grandeur. But hark! What's that roaring? Ah, it's our dramatist. He's his own playwright and his own player. Although he sometimes appears to be quite beside himself, he never loses his composure, for his dignity is inborn. Dignity, then, and at the same time wildness. Just think how beautiful and majestic it is when he sleeps. But let's have a look at him when he senses the approach of feeding time. He descends to the level of an impatient child, in love with the vision of the approaching feast. Then at least he has something to do: he can tear at fresh meat. He's so good at eating. How oddly a caged animal like this must know—and to some extent love—his keeper. At rest, how divine he is. He appears to be in mourning, appears to be entertaining quite particular thoughts, and I am tempted to swear that the thoughts he is immersed in are beautiful and sublime. Have you ever

let him have a good look at you? Try it, attract his attention some-
time. His gaze is the gaze of a god. And then what is he like when he
grows uneasy and strides up and down in his prison cell, pressing his
princely strength against the walls of his cage. Always up and down.
Up and down. For hours on end. What a scene! Up and down, and
his powerful tail thrashes the ground.

1910

BERLIN LIFE

BERLIN AND THE ARTIST

ELSEWHERE, in the quiet provinces, the artist can easily find himself surrounded by melancholias. Lost in thought, he sits at the secluded window of his medieval digs, a strange twilight flowing all about him, and without so much as stirring he sends his daydreams out into the sweeping landscape. No one comes. Nothing disturbs his reverie. An inexpressible silence rules the surrounds. In the capital, on the other hand, there is no dearth of disturbances, it's like a lively warehouse of good cheer, and naturally this is something our man finds beneficial. The souls of artists must always be woken a little from the magic spell in which they lie fettered. Inside almost every artist—certainly in every true one—lies a fairy-tale realm. In the land of fairy tales, however, a great deal of slumbering occurs. One doesn't stir much. Are not today's German provinces much like a dreaming, slumbering fairy tale? Magdeburg, for instance. Does Magdeburg possess its own self-sufficient and self-assured intellectual life? Not particularly. That's the problem.

Berlin, by comparison—how splendid! A city like Berlin is an ill-mannered, impertinent, intelligent scoundrel, constantly affirming the things that suit him and tossing aside everything he tires of. Here in the big city you can definitely feel the waves of intellect washing over the life of Berlin society like a sort of bath. An artist here has no choice but to pay attention. Elsewhere he is permitted to stop up his ears and sink into willful ignorance. Here this is not allowed. Rather, he must constantly pull himself together as a human being, and this compulsion encircling him redounds to his advantage. But there are yet other things as well.

Berlin never rests, and this is glorious. Each dawning day brings with it a new, agreeably disagreeable attack on complacency, and this does the general sense of indolence good. An artist possesses, much like a child, an inborn propensity for beautiful, noble slug-gardizing. Well, this slug-a-beddishness, this kingdom, is constantly being buffeted by fresh storm-winds of inspiration. The refined, si-lent creature is suddenly blustered full of something coarse, loud, and unrefined. There is an incessant blurring together of various things, and this is good, this is Berlin, and Berlin is outstanding.

The excellent gentleman from the provinces, however, should by no means imagine that here in the city there are not lonelinesses as well. The metropolis contains lonelinesses of the most frightful sort, and anyone who wishes to sample this exquisite dish can eat his fill of it here. He can experience what it means to live in deserts and wastes. The metropolitan artist has no dearth of opportunities to see and speak to no one at all. All he has to do is make himself unpopu-lar among certain arbiters of taste or else consistently fixate on fail-ures, and in no time he'll have sunk into the most splendid, most blossoming of abandonments.

The artist who is crowned with success lives in the metropolis as if in an enchanting Oriental dream. He hastens from one elegant household to the affluent next, sits down unhesitatingly at the opu-lently laden dining tables, and while chewing and slurping provides the entertainment. He passes his days in a virtual state of intoxica-tion. And his talent? Does an artist such as this neglect his talent? What a question! As if one might cast off one's gifts without so much as a by-your-leave. On the contrary. Talent unconsciously grows stronger when one throws oneself into life. You mustn't be constantly tending and coddling it like a sickly something. It shriv-els up when it's too timidly cared for.

The artistic individual is nonetheless permitted to pace up and down, like a tiger, in his cave of artistic creation, mad with desire and worry over achieving some output of beauty. As no one sees this, there is no one to hold it against him. In company, he should be as breezy, affable, and charming as he can manage, neither too self-important nor too unimportant either. One thing he must never forget: he is all but required to pay court to beautiful, wealthy women at least a little.

After approximately five or six years have passed, the artist—even if he comes from peasant stock—will feel at home in the metropolis. His parents would appear to have lived and given birth to him here. He feels indebted, bound, and beholden to this strange rattling, clattering racket. All the scurrying and fluttering about now seem to him a sort of nebulous, beloved maternal figure. He no longer thinks of ever leaving again. Whether things go well with him or poorly, whether he comes down in the world or flourishes, no matter, it "has" him, he is forever under its spell, and it would be impossible for him to bid this magnificent restlessness adieu.

1910

KUTSCH

OF KUTSCH it is known that he has three unfinished plays in his armoire, besides which he's at work on a fourth, using material borrowed from Maupassant.

Hey there, Kutsch!

Kutsch finds it distasteful to be so flippantly addressed, he's distrustful and perhaps has good cause for this, as he is striving for ultimate greatness, and all who strive for greatness aren't so keen on rubbing shoulders with their fellow man.

People of this sort are always envisioning a certain far-off something. Such individuals find themselves constantly faced with the necessity that whispers to them: Evolve!—Kutsch needs to evolve, it's at the top of his list, and this same uncanny force is always tormenting him a little, making him prick up his ears and commanding that he assume a stricken, nervous facial expression.

He has long, narrow hands, sensitive hands. Certain satirical illustrators like nothing better than to have a go at such hands to exploit them in their drawings. My intention here is to offer up a serious character study, and since this is the case it is crucial to pay very close attention to ensure that no feature appears in exaggerated form.

Colleague Kutsch!

This is a word he's not terribly fond of, he'd prefer not to be anyone's colleague, he's a sort of up-high person always tugging his collar up about his ears. When you give his hand a good squeeze, it makes a cracking sound, and when he's wearing his hat, he has a quite interesting head.

He's constantly afraid people might be poking fun at him, but there are certain individuals you cannot faithfully portray without poking a bit of fun.

One night Kutsch left a hastily penned drama lying in the coffeehouse, on one of those coffeehouse sofas upon which the habitual aesthete is wont to fling himself down to sip coffee and stare into space. Some other fellow found the play, picked it up, put it in his pocket, brought it home, copied it over, completed it, prepared it for staging, and then had it put on in a first-rate theater, where it was a success.

This one too was based on a story by Maupassant. Yes, indeed. In the work of Maupassant, that loutish peasant from Normandy, great quantities of "Life" are stored away, anyone who's read him must surely have noticed this.

Kutsch studies his subject matter rather than life itself; the life he has heretofore experienced still leaves much to be desired. He writes for the papers and reviews books, that's what he's experienced, and this, in his opinion, is not particularly striking as experiences go.

What a shame he wasn't born in—let's say for example—the time of Louis XIV in France; surely he'd have shown some of those brilliant scalawags just having their heyday at the time what he was capable of.

The thing is: Kutsch can do anything, and he wants everything too, but in fact he does nothing at all. He writes critiques of novels because he himself is an epic author through and through; he reviews plays because he himself is thoroughly possessed by the devil of this discipline; and he writes about poetry because he himself ought to have written some poems if only he'd wanted to.

He'll be angry when he reads this. I shall say to him: Here, take this! And shall press into his hand the modest, though for him not negligible, honorarium I shall have received for this sketch.

Sometimes those who poke fun have the extravagant habit of being philanthropic.

My God, Kutsch is so impoverished, so abandoned by all the world. Keep in mind that he strives only for what is noble and first-rate. He is not merely a person like any other, just as most people are not merely people like any other.

I, however, most definitely number among the hundred thousand. I am virtually indistinguishable from a household servant, and am glad to be so ordinary.

Did you catch the undercurrent of vindictive envy?

Why should I envy Kutsch? On the contrary, I pity him. After all, I'm writing an essay on him, and so I must of necessity feel he is beneath me, since otherwise I could hardly be writing "on" him.

This ignoble practice of just going and writing about living human beings as though they were dead. And then this Kutsch isn't even interesting, I hear the reader protest.

1907

FABULOUS

THE WEATHER was fabulous. On such a splendid day, Kitsch and Kutsch had no desire to stay home, and so they readied themselves to go out and then hurried down to the street. Fabulous, this light in the street, Kutsch murmured as the two of them marched vigorously forward, and Kitsch as well said: Fabulous. Soon a plump woman came walking toward them, and at once this woman was declared fabulous by the two promenaders. They boarded the "electric"— how utterly fabulous, Kutsch opined once more, scratching at his youthful beard, riding along like this, and Kitsch lost no time in agreeing emphatically with his companion. A girl with "fabulous eyes" was sitting in the car. Suddenly a light rain began to fall: Fabulous!

After a while our Kitsch and Kutsch got out again and went to an art salon. The art dealer was looking out the window of his shop, and this nearly appeared fabulous to the two of them, which would have gone like this: How fabulous, the way this fellow is looking out his shop window. But they avoided giving spoken expression to this thought because they sensed it wasn't right to always go on saying exactly the same thing. Half a minute later they were standing before a Renoir: Simply fabulous! shot out of their mouths. Kutsch once more began to scrape away at his beard with his fingers, but already his colleague had discovered something that was a full ten fables more fabulous than the Renoir, namely an old Dutch artist. Something like this, they said, was more than fabulous, and both of them felt like shouting.

Then they departed. Outdoors meanwhile a fine crust of snow

had fallen, quite fabulous-looking; the snow was so black, a bluish black, it was simply—well, they contained themselves, after all you don't always want to go on saying exactly the same thing. They ran into a painter. It wasn't long before the painter was telling them that he knew nothing more fabulous than Paris. Kitsch and Kutsch found it distasteful to go about saying that Paris was fabulous, and soon they were treating this unsuspecting painter and his fee-fi-fo-fum-fabulous Paris with contempt. As soon as they were alone once more, things started right back up again, but they found it appropriate; this time it was a pond. They stood upon a bridge, and there below them lay the pond in all its fabulousness. All at once they spoke of poems by Verlaine—Kutsch clapped his hands and cried: Fabulous. Then Kitsch started smiling. Now he'd figured it out, he said to himself: How base it was to go on fabulousing like that at every paltry opportunity. One minute later he crumpled to the ground, felled by the fabulous sight of a woman's blue skirt. That blue is magnificent, Kitsch said, getting to his feet again with effort. He'd twisted his ankle. And from this moment on they always used the word magnificent, never again fabulous.

1907

MOUNTAIN HALLS

DO YOU know the mountain halls on Unter den Linden? Perhaps you'll try going there someday. The price of admission is a mere thirty cents. Even if you see the cashier eating bread or sausage, you needn't turn away in disgust, instead just take into account that it's her supper she's eating. Nature demands its rights everywhere. Wherever Nature is found, there is meaning. And now you'll step inside, going into the mountains. And here you will encounter a huge figure, a sort of Rübezahl or mountain spirit—he's the publican here, and you'll do well to salute him by doffing your hat. He appreciates such gestures, and he'll thank you courteously for your politeness by half rising from the chair on which he sits. Flattered in your soul, you now approach the glacier, which is the stage: a geological, geographical, and architectural curiosity. As soon as you've sat down, you'll receive a drink proposal tendered by a perhaps moderately pretty waitress. Well, no use being dissatisfied with what's available. Even on theater nights, there may be no great abundance here of feminine charms. Watch out that not too many glasses of apple wine sloshed and splashed to the brim are grouped about your paying person. The girls are all too quick to attach themselves to gentlemen who pity them. Pity is unsuitable when it's a matter of artistic enjoyment. Have you been attending to the performance of this dancer? Kleist too waited many years for recognition. Go ahead and applaud valiantly, even if it almost displeased you. Now, what have you done with your alpenstock? Left it at home? Next time, for better or worse, you'll have to come properly equipped when you head to the mountains, just in case. One cannot be too careful. And who is this ravishing alpine-shepherd's-hut princess now approaching with dainty step? It's the resident sweet young thing, and she's hoping you'll treat her to a walloped-full glass of beer to the tune of fifty cents. Will you be able to resist these lips, these eyes, this sweet, foolish request? You'd be lamentable if you could. Now the crevasse in the glacier-stage opens once more before you, and a Danish songstress sprinkles you with notes and snowflakes of grace. You're just taking a sip of your cow-warm mountain milk. The publican is making his watchful bouncer rounds through the establishment. He sees to decorum and proper behavior. Do pay the place a visit, why don't you, eh? You might even meet me again someday there. But I shan't even recognize you. It's my habit to sit there in silence, under a magic spell. I quench my thirst, melodies rock me to sleep, I dream.

1908

THE LITTLE BERLINER

PAPA BOXED my ears today, in a most fond and fatherly manner, of course. I had used the expression: "Father, you must be nuts." It was indeed a bit careless of me. "Ladies should employ exquisite language," our German teacher says. She's horrible. But Papa won't allow me to ridicule her, and perhaps he's right. After all, one does go to school to exhibit a certain zeal for learning and a certain respect. Besides, it is cheap and vulgar to discover funny things in a fellow human being and then to laugh at them. Young ladies should accustom themselves to the fine and the noble—I quite see that. No one desires any work from me, no one will ever demand it of me; but everyone will expect to find that I am refined in my ways. Shall I enter some profession in later life? Of course not! I'll be an elegant young wife; I shall get married. It is possible that I'll torment my husband. But that would be terrible. One always despises oneself whenever one feels the need to despise someone else. I am twelve years old. I must be very precocious—otherwise, I would never think of such things. Shall I have children? And how will that come about? If my future husband isn't a despicable human being, then, yes, then I'm sure of it, I shall have a child. Then I shall bring up this child. But I still have to be brought up myself. What silly thoughts one can have!

Berlin is the most beautiful, the most cultivated city in the world. I would be detestable if I weren't unshakably convinced of this. Doesn't the Kaiser live here? Would he need to live here if he didn't like it here best of all? The other day I saw the royal children in an open car. They are enchanting. The crown prince looks like a high-spirited young god, and how beautiful seemed the noble lady at his side. She was completely hidden in fragrant furs. It seemed that blossoms rained down upon the pair out of the blue sky. The Tiergarten is marvelous. I go walking there almost every day with our young lady, the governess. One can go for hours under the green trees, on straight or winding paths. Even Father, who doesn't really need to be enthusiastic about anything, is enthusiastic about the Tiergarten. Father is a cultivated man. I'm convinced he loves me madly. It would be horrible if he read this, but I shall tear up what I have written. Actually, it is not at all fitting to be still so silly and immature and, at the same time, already want to keep a diary. But, from time to time, one becomes somewhat bored, and then one easily gives way to what is not quite right. The governess is very nice. Well, I mean, in general. She is devoted and she loves me. In addition, she has real respect for Papa—that is the most important thing. She is slender of figure. Our previous governess was fat as a frog. She always seemed to be about to burst. She was English. She's still English today, of course, but from the moment she allowed herself liberties, she was no longer our concern. Father kicked her out.

The two of us, Papa and I, are soon to take a trip. It is that time of the year now when respectable people simply have to take a trip. Isn't it a suspicious sort of person who doesn't take a trip at such a time of blossoming and blooming? Papa goes to the seashore and apparently lies there day after day and lets himself be baked dark brown by the summer sun. He always looks healthiest in September. The paleness of exhaustion is not becoming to his face. Incidentally, I myself love the suntanned look in a man's face. It is as if he had just come home from war. Isn't that just like a child's nonsense? Well, I'm still a child, of course. As far as I'm concerned, I'm taking a trip to the south. First of all, a little while to Munich and then to Venice, where a person who is unspeakably close to me lives—Mama. For reasons whose depths I cannot understand and consequently cannot evaluate, my parents live apart. Most of the time I live with Father. But naturally Mother also has the right to possess me at least for a while. I can scarcely wait for the approaching trip. I like to travel, and I think that almost all people must like to travel. One boards the train, it departs, and off it goes into the distance. One sits and is carried into the remote unknown. How well-off I am, really! What do I know of need, of poverty? Nothing at all. I also don't find it the least bit necessary that I should experience anything so base. But I do feel sorry for the poor children. I would jump out the window under such conditions.

Papa and I reside in the most elegant quarter of the city. Quarters which are quiet, scrupulously clean, and fairly old, are elegant. The brand-new? I wouldn't like to live in a brand-new house. In new things there is always something which isn't quite in order. One sees hardly any poor people—for example, workers—in our neighborhood, where the houses have their own gardens. The people who live in our vicinity are factory owners, bankers, and wealthy people whose profession is wealth. So Papa must be, at the very least, quite well-to-do. The poor and the poorish people simply can't live around here because the apartments are much too expensive. Papa says that the class ruled by misery lives in the north of the city. What a city! What is it—the north? I know Moscow better than I know the north of our city. I have been sent numerous postcards from Moscow, Petersburg, Vladivostok, and Yokohama. I know the beaches of Belgium and Holland; I know the Engadine with its sky-high mountains and its green meadows, but my own city? Perhaps to many, many people who inhabit it, Berlin remains a mystery. Papa supports art and the artists. What he engages in is business. Well, lords often engage in business, too, and then Papa's dealings are of absolute refinement. He buys and sells paintings. We have very beautiful paintings in our house. The point of Father's business, I think, is this: the artists, as a rule, understand nothing about business, or, for some reason or other, they aren't allowed to understand anything about it. Or it is this: the world is big and coldhearted. The world never thinks about the existence of artists. That's where my father comes in, worldly-wise, with all sorts of important connections, and in suitable and clever fashion, he draws the attention of this world, which has perhaps no need at all for art, to art and to artists who are starving. Father often looks down upon his buyers. But he often looks down upon the artists, too. It all depends.

No, I wouldn't want to live permanently anywhere but in Berlin. Do the children in small towns, towns that are old and decayed, live any better? Of course, there are some things there that we don't have. Romantic things? I believe I'm not mistaken when I look upon something that is scarcely half alive as romantic. The defective, the crumbled, the diseased; e.g., an ancient city wall. Whatever is useless yet mysteriously beautiful—that is romantic. I love to dream about such things, and, as I see it, dreaming about them is enough. Ultimately, the most romantic thing is the heart, and every sensitive person carries in himself old cities enclosed by ancient walls. Our Berlin will soon burst at the seams with newness. Father says that everything historically notable here will vanish; no one knows the old Berlin anymore. Father knows everything, or at least, almost everything. And naturally his daughter profits in that respect. Yes, little towns laid out in the middle of the countryside may well be nice. There would be charming, secret hiding spots to play in, caves to crawl in, meadows, fields, and, only a few steps away, the forest. Such villages seem to be wreathed in green; but Berlin has an Ice Palace where people ice-skate on the hottest summer day. Berlin is simply one step ahead of all other German cities, in every respect. It is the cleanest, most modern city in the world. Who says this? Well, Papa, of course. How good he is, really! I have much to learn from him. Our Berlin streets have overcome all dirt and all bumps. They are as smooth as ice and they glisten like scrupulously polished floors. Nowadays one sees a few people roller-skating. Who knows, perhaps I'll be doing it someday, too, if it hasn't already gone out of fashion. There are fashions here that scarcely have time to come in properly. Last year all the children, and also many grown-ups, played Diabolo. Now this game is out of fashion, no one wants to play it. That's how everything changes. Berlin always sets the fashion. No one is obliged to imitate, and yet Madam Imitation is the great and exalted ruler of this life. Everyone imitates.

Papa can be charming, actually, he is always nice, but at times he becomes angry about something—one never knows—and then he is ugly. I can see in him how secret anger, just like discontent, makes people ugly. If Papa isn't in a good mood, I feel as cowed as a whipped dog, and therefore Papa should avoid displaying his indisposition and his discontent to his associates, even if they should consist of only one daughter. There, yes, precisely there, fathers commit sins. I sense it vividly. But who doesn't have weaknesses—not even one, not some tiny fault? Who is without sin? Parents who don't consider it necessary to withhold their personal storms from their children degrade them to slaves in no time. A father should overcome his bad moods in private—but how difficult that is!—or he should take them to strangers. A daughter is a young lady, and in every cultivated sire should dwell a cavalier. I say explicitly: living with Father is like Paradise, and if I discover a flaw in him, doubtless it is one transferred from him to me; thus it is his, not my, discretion that observes him closely. But Papa may, of course, conveniently take out his anger on people who are dependent on him in certain respects. There are enough such people fluttering about him.

I have my own room, my furniture, my luxury, my books, etc. God, I'm actually very well provided for. Am I thankful to Papa for all this? What a tasteless question! I am obedient to him, and then I am also his possession, and, in the last analysis, he can well be proud of me. I cause him worries, I am his financial concern, he may snap at me, and I always find it a kind of delicate obligation to laugh at him when he snaps at me. Papa likes to snap; he has a sense of humor and is, at the same time, spirited. At Christmas he overwhelms me with presents. Incidentally, my furniture was designed by an artist who is scarcely unknown. Father deals almost exclusively with people who have some sort of name. He deals with names. If hidden in such a name there is also a man, so much the better. How horrible it must be to know that one is famous and to feel that one doesn't deserve it at all. I can imagine many such famous people. Isn't such a fame like an incurable sickness? Goodness, the way I express myself! My furniture is lacquered white and is painted with flowers and fruits by the hands of a connoisseur. They are charming and the artist who painted them is a remarkable person, highly esteemed by Father. And whomever Father esteems should indeed be flattered. I mean, it is worth something if Papa is well-disposed toward someone, and those who don't find it so and act as if they didn't give a hoot, they're only hurting themselves. They don't see the world clearly enough. I consider my father to be a thoroughly remarkable man, that he wields influence in the world is obvious.—Many of my books bore me. But then they are simply not the right books, like, for example, so-called children's books. Such books are an affront. One dares give children books to read that don't go beyond their horizons? One should not speak in a childlike manner to children; it is childish. I, who am still a child myself, hate childishness.

When shall I cease to amuse myself with toys? No, toys are sweet, and I shall be playing with my doll for a long time yet; but I play consciously. I know that it's silly, but how beautiful silly and useless things are. Artistic natures, I think, must feel the same way. Different young artists often come to us, that is to say, to Papa, for dinner. Well, they are invited and then they appear. Often I write the invitations, often the governess, and a grand, entertaining liveliness reigns at our table, which, without boasting or willfully showing off, looks like the well-provided table of a fine house. Papa apparently enjoys going around with young people, with people who are younger than he, and yet he is always the gayest and the youngest. One hears him talking most of the time, the others listen, or they allow themselves little remarks, which is often quite droll. Father over-towers them all in learning and verve and understanding of the world, and all these people learn from him—that I plainly see. Often I have to laugh at the table; then I receive a gentle or not-so-gentle admonition. Yes, and then after dinner we take it easy. Papa stretches out on the leather sofa and begins to snore, which actually is in rather poor taste. But I'm in love with Papa's behavior. Even his candid snoring pleases me. Does one want to, could one ever, make conversation all the time?

Father apparently spends a lot of money. He has receipts and expenses, he lives, he strives after gains, he lets live. He even leans a bit toward extravagance and waste. He's constantly in motion. "Clearly he's one of those people who find it a pleasure and, yes, even a necessity, to constantly take risks." At our house there is much said about success and failure. Whoever eats with us and associates with us has attained some form of smaller or greater success in the world. What is the world? A rumor, a topic of conversation? In any case, my father stands in the very middle of this topic of conversation. Perhaps he even directs it, within certain bounds. Papa's aim, at all events, is to wield power. He attempts to develop, to assert both himself and those people in whom he has an interest. His principle is: He in whom I have no interest damages himself. As a result of this view, Father is always permeated with a healthy sense of his human worth and can step forth, firm and certain, as is fitting. Whoever grants himself no importance feels no qualms about perpetrating bad deeds. What am I talking about? Did I hear Father say that?

Have I the benefit of a good upbringing? I refuse even to doubt it. I have been brought up as a metropolitan lady should be brought up, with familiarity and, at the same time, with a certain measured severity, which permits and, at the same time, commands me to accustom myself to tact. The man who is to marry me must be rich, or he must have substantial prospects of an assured prosperity. Poor? I couldn't be poor.

It is impossible for me and for creatures like me to suffer pecuniary need. That would be stupid. In other respects, I shall be certain to give simplicity preference in my mode of living. I do not like outward display. Simplicity must be a luxury.

It must shimmer with propriety in every respect, and such refinements of life, brought to perfection, cost money. The amenities are expensive. How energetically I'm talking now! Isn't it a bit imprudent? Shall I love? What is love? What sorts of strange and wonderful things must yet await me if I find myself so unknowing about things that I'm still too young to understand. What experiences shall I have?

1909
Translated by Harriet Watts

FLOWER DAYS

ON CORNFLOWER Day, when everyone struts around in blue, it became evident how much the writer of the present scientific treatise feels himself to be a good, innocent child of his times. Indeed, I have participated in each and every nice and nasty cornflower folly with joy, love, and delight, and I must have behaved, I believe, very funnily. Several proud and earnest nonparticipants cast severe looks in my direction, but me, happy me, I was as if intoxicated, and I made a pilgrimage, I must confess, while blushing, from one distillery to the next, while buying, all along the way from Münzstrasse to Motzstrasse, patriotic flowers. Clad in blue from head to foot, I seemed to myself most graceful, but what is more, I felt myself most vividly to be a respectable member of the upper classes. Oh, this sweet feeling, how it befogged me and how happy it makes me, the beautiful, yes perhaps even, depending on circumstances, noble thought that I might fling to left and right, with very graceful gestures, pennies, healthy, true, honest, honorable, well-behaved, good pennies, thereby accomplishing a goodly work. Now come what may, let it happen to me, poor devil that I am: I am pleased with myself, thoroughly so, and a feeling of peace has overcome me, I cannot express it in carefully chosen or unchosen words. In my hand, or fist, I held a thick, huge, and evidently imposing bouquet of freshly picked paper flowers, the fragrance of which captivated me. I discovered, by the way, that such flowers are sold at seven pennies a dozen. A waiter, as honest as he is stupid, who always says "Very well" when he takes an order, told me this in a series of mysterious whispers. I am always on an intimate footing with waiters and suchlike people. That's just by the way.

As for flower days in general, I would have to be a heartless rascal not to grasp at once the noble purport on which they rest, and therefore I leap forward as rapidly as possible and exclaim aloud: Yes, it is true, flower days are heavenly. They are not comical in the least, but have, to my feeling, a thoroughly noble and earnest character. Among us blokes or fellow beings, of course, there are still a few isolated and, it would seem, obstinate people who would scorn to wear, on a flower day, a day of peace and joy, a pleasure flower in their soul-buttonhole. We might hope that such people may soon learn better and nobler ways. As for me, as I may fortunately declare, I am radiant on flower days, with sheer flowery and flowerish satisfaction, and I am one of the most flower-encrusted persons among all those who are beautified, adorned, and beflowered. In a word, on such a Day of Plants I am like a swaying, tender plant, and on the charming Violet Day that soon is coming I shall, this I know for certain, appear in the world myself as a modest and secluded violet. For some magnanimous purpose I might even be able to transform myself into a daisy. In future, let anyone, I would here heartily plead, stick and wedge his buttercup between his lips, whether they be opened or grimly tight shut. Ears, too, are excellent props for flowers. On Cornflower Day I had stuck a cornflower behind each of my three ears, and it was most becoming. Ravishing, too, are roses, and the Rose Days soon to come. Let them descend upon me, those distinctive days, and I shall embellish my home with roses, and, sure as I'm a modern man and understand my epoch, I shall stick a rose in my nose. I can warm to Daisy Days most animatedly too, since any random fashion, absolutely any, makes of me a servant, a slave, or subject. Yet I am happy so.

Well, even then, such odd people, who lack character, have also to exist. The main thing is: I mean to enjoy my morsel of life as well and as long as I can, and if a person finds it amusing he'll heartily go along with any kind of nonsense; but now I turn to the most beautiful subject of all—to women. For them, for them alone, the gracious flower days were invented, composed, poeticized. If a man wallows in flowers, it's a bit unnatural; but in every way it befits a woman to put flowers in her hair and bring flowers to a man. Such a lady or virgin flower has only to make a sign, a gesture, and at once I hurl myself at her feet, ask her, my whole body trembling with joy, how much the flower costs, and I buy it from her. Then all pale in the face I breathe a glowing kiss upon her roguish little hand, and am prepared to surrender my life for her. Yes, indeed, in this manner, and others to match, I do behave on flower days. From time to time, to refresh myself, I plunge, it is true, into a snack hall and gulp down, there and then, a potted-meat sandwich. I adore potted meat, but I adore flowers too. There are now many things that I adore. All the same, one has to do one's duty as a citizen, nobody should make a face, nobody think he has a right to pass the flower days off with a quiet smile. They are a fact of life; but one should respect facts. Should one really?

1911
Translated by Christopher Middleton

FIRE

EVEN IN a large city, the streets after a certain advanced hour of night are relatively still. What one hears and sees are apparitions and sounds to which both our eyes and our ears have long since grown accustomed. There are none of the usual sounds. People are at home, sitting around the cozy family table, or else in bars hunkered over their beers and political discussions, or in the concert hall, reverently listening to the pieces of music being performed, or at the theater, following the suspenseful goings-on upon the brightly lit stage, or else they are standing in pairs, or in groups of three or seven on some melancholy street corner, delving into profundities, or else perhaps aimlessly walking in some direction or other. "Hey there, car!" another cries out, and somewhere there might be a poet buried in his isolated room, drunkards wandering in wretched bliss from one still to another, bawling and harassing the passersby; perhaps a horse pulling a hackney cab is collapsing somewhere, a woman fainting, a scoundrel being apprehended by the always vigilant and safety-restoring police force—and suddenly someone shouts: "*Fire!*" Quite close by, it seems, a fire has broken out. People were just standing around, indecisive and bored, about to accuse the hour of lacking all interest and in any case starting to feel chilled, and suddenly here's this great novelty being presented, something unexpected to kindle our enthusiasm. Everyone lurches forward and without realizing it has already begun a conversation with whoever happens to be standing alongside, cheeks are glowing, and now people are even starting to leap and run. They're suddenly doing something they haven't tried in a good two years. All at once the world appears changed, expanded, thicker, and more tangible.

A metropolis is a giant spiderweb of squares, streets, bridges, buildings, gardens, and wide, long avenues. When a fire breaks out, only the neighbors closest to the scene of the fire know of the conflagration. Indeed, in a huge city like this there can be three, four, or even five large fires in the course of a single night, far apart from one another, each one representing a disaster in its own right, an "event," without one having even the slightest impact on the others: five suspenseful chapters of a novel, each of them self-contained, without links to the other. A metropolis is a wave-filled ocean that for the most part is still largely unknown to its own inhabitants, an impenetrable forest, an opulent, overgrown, huge, forgotten, or half-forgotten park, a thing that has been built up too extensively for it to ever again be oriented within itself. But now dozens of people are hurriedly racing to the scene of the fire. They now know approximately where the blaze is.

And now you turn a corner and the fire is right in front of you, it looks as if it wants to leap forward to greet you; an entire street is brightly, garishly lit up by it, it resembles a sunset in the distant south, ten evenings ablaze, a host of suns setting in unison. You see the façades of buildings looking like pale-yellow paper, and the bright red glow of the fire approaches, a thick, glowing, wounded red, and beside it the street lanterns look like feebly burning damp matches. And cries ring out. It seems as if trumpets are sounding everywhere, but this is a false impression, everything is relatively quiet, it's just that you are running, and beside you, before you and behind, others are now loping as well, and hackney cabs are trotting past, and the electric tram passes by. There is something ordinary about all of this, yet at the same time something incomprehensible. Suddenly everyone stops short as if standing before a fairy tale. What now appears resembles a bomb effect dreamed up by an enterprising theater director.

A thick, seemingly incessant rain of small, light sparks and embers flies out of the dark air and down into the crowded street, sowing a crop of glowing snow. At just this moment a commuter train rolls past, and it too is soon entirely covered with this peculiar snow. People are standing there incautiously gazing up into the red-dotted sky without considering that a glowing, scalding hot snowflake might strike them in the eye. The coat of a gentleman who is just riding past on the tram catches fire. This tiny conflagration, however, causes no serious harm. Still it goes on raining in this unfamiliar, unprecedented way. Involuntarily you sense how very fortunate you are to still be capable of believing in a miracle out of the *Thousand and One Nights*. And indeed: we feel we have suddenly been transported to the Orient and the Arabian nights when we glimpse, right in front of us, a rosily shimmering fairy palace. It is perhaps a building whose architecture has been repeatedly criticized. But at this moment it isn't clear which is more deserving of admiration: the charm of the Venetian illumination or the unsurpassedly beautiful architecture. This fiery glow is the consummate architect.

You find yourself being shoved this way and that, half lifted up, carried along and rocked. An immense crowd has assembled all around this roaring, hissing, flickering fire catastrophe. Will lives be lost? people wonder. Soon all are finding the throng as familiar as an intimate friendship with a dear, admirable person. Now and again hot fiery winds blow across people's faces, new flurries of sparks rise in the air, a splendid sight. And still it burns, and so and so many people are taking in the spectacle of the flames. One or the other is about to leave, but once again his eye is drawn back to the fire, irresistibly. If you now stand up high on your toes, you can see constables on horseback. "We were just expecting you," some young fellow remarks. Others laugh. Everyone is standing head to head, breath beside breath, feeling beside feeling, curiosity beside curiosity, body to body, and each of them still finds himself compelled to go on reading this suspenseful nature story. Automobiles in the midst of the pressing crowd. "Let's go stand somewhere else. This corner gives me the creeps." Words of this sort are heard. Suddenly a majestic flaming figure bursts forth from a glowing gap in the conflagration, a veritable fiery giant, and thrusts itself far out into the night air, taking the form of gently falling rain, as though something beautiful and huge was just there and now is dying out.

More and more people keep arriving as others leave. Those departing throw themselves amusingly into the wake of the puffing, tootling cars, which helpfully bore a path through the malleable throng, making their departure possible. The electric trams are stuffed to bursting because of all the many people taking refuge in the cars. Other inquisitive faces peer out the windows of nearby buildings. And now even the elegant nocturnal party set is sending out its envoys, both female and male, bedded in hackney cabs and furs, and still the fire continues to rage. The fire's wrath is not so easily placated, not even with streams of water, even the most sustained. You see the team of firefighters, admiring the daredevil positions they assume, yet cannot help expecting at every moment to see them succumb to smoke and flames. Now a general jostling ensues: policemen up front are pushing back the crowd! It's difficult to keep your footing, and in the first uncertainty of your new position you grasp, as if to steady yourself, the nearest available hand, which happens to be the delightful hand of a girl, but then, like it or not, this property must be let go of.

Is this a great calamity? Thanks to the vigilance and valor of the fire department, the extent of the loss has been reduced, but an old, memorable, venerable building has been lost, and this is loss enough. Enough charming sites from ancient times have been snatched from us by everyday life and its raucous demands, and now the fire too is helping to thin out Berlin's statues and historical monuments. But the populace is not terribly concerned with all that "old rubbish." A postman standing there among the crowd remarks that it's good to have room for new things. In Berlin, he adds, things are getting too cramped anyhow—it's terrible how it blocks the flow of traffic. A person has to head for Charlottenburg—now there's a proper region where you can find wide, lovely, bright streets, etc.

My companion is now urging me on, he's cold, and both of us are meanwhile convinced that we are hungry for a nice supper. We leave, but keep turning around to look back again. The yellow, red, glowing entity behind us is still alive, displaying frightful vitality, still speaking this same fierce, furious language, still feeling the same indestructible incendiary sentiments. But my companion declares it's getting tedious to watch the flames for so long. I concede the point. It is one of my possibly bad habits that I am constantly conceding points to my fellow man.

1908

SOMETHING ABOUT THE RAILWAY

HOW NICE it is to stand about in train stations and in a leisurely fashion observe the travelers who are arriving and going off again. Many a poor, destitute devil enjoys this pastime, for it is an amusement that costs nothing at all. Nor does it require any formalities or rules; you merely stand there, your hands possibly in your trouser pockets, a cigarette or cigar stump in your mouth, almost indecorously, and yet without attracting any particular notice, and in this way you may enjoy the liveliest and loveliest spectacle in the world, for this is a train station. Train stations in the countryside can be downright ravishing with their gardens and the little stands of trees that tend to be situated beside such buildings, but in the train stations of royal seats and capitals there's more going on, and all this mobility is sometimes far more beautiful than all beautiful, peaceful landscapes. For the unemployed and all the various sorts of idlers that today's industrial, artistic, and commercial life and activity at times sets out on the street, train stations and the sight of the departing and arriving trains are ideal. The ne'er-do-well has plenty of time at his disposal, and as a result he observes practically everything, he walks slowly up and down the smooth platforms, measuring out steps of noble elegance, and lets his eyes wander everywhere. What a great massing and intermingling! At the ticket windows there are often veritable public assemblies and imperiously demanding mobs, as though we found ourselves in a year of passionate revolution. Everyone wants to receive his ticket as quickly as possible, but usually he has failed to sort out the exact change in advance as admonished by the station's solicitous management. The idler is better off: he need not run and need not fear that the express train will pull out right under his nose. "I was just about to get on when, so help me God, that black devil of a train took off right past my hat." This is the sort of thing uttered by travelers with boarding intentions, but not by the person whose aim it is to blithely, quietly observe. What a pushing, pressing, shoving, racing mayhem! Ah, here's an important train pulling in, and you stand there watching how they throw their arms about each other's necks, how kisses are distributed left and right, how hats are waved about, how the charming heads of women blush, how hands and arms are held out to receive, how eyes light up, how servants awaiting their masters stand to attention as they catch sight of them and then swiftly relieve them of their little suitcases, packages, and all sorts of silly items.

After two or three minutes the hubbub generally dies down, and the idler takes up position somewhere else. There is always something happening everywhere in a train station, he's quite aware of this, and so he is not at all concerned he might have cause to suffer tedium. Not a bit of it. He goes into the third-, fourth-, sixth-, or, as far as he cares, fourteenth-class restaurant, where there are always people sitting about on the benches or chairs or at tables. He's already accustomed to the unsavory odors to be found in such establishments, and so nothing could possibly shrink or incinerate his pleasure. The twine he's used to bind his enjoyment to this spectacle holds firm, and now perhaps he drinks a glass of beer and converses with an honest traveling journeyman who's sitting on his suitcase as though he were afraid someone might come along and rob him of all he owns. From time to time the loiterer might venture into the first- and second-class waiting rooms so as to pay a visit, if only a brief and rather conspicuous one, to the elegance and luxury that has settled itself here in lordly comfort. Sometimes he's chased off by a stern official wearing a railway uniform, but this does him no harm, after all, he has once again beheld something beautiful with his eyes! If he is well-dressed, he might secretly sit down here among the aristocracy and the bankers' guild and order a cognac which he will drink intelligently and with pensive dignity while striking up a conversation with a pretty waitress clad in a folksy Oberland costume. "Express train departing for Milan in four minutes," a by all appearances courteous employee announces; our man rises to his feet, pays his tab, and strolls casually out to have a look at this Milan departure. What excellent grooming, what ensembles! Many of the ladies boarding the train wear white veils on their hats, and their cavaliers assist them with greater or lesser degrees of skill as they get in. The train chugs off, a few handkerchiefs are waved about like little flags, the ne'er-do-well is himself departing in his thoughts, in other words he imagines sitting in an empty compartment, reading a newspaper.

But for the moment begone with this loitering observer, whose experiences in the end are after all rather one-sided. All at once we really are sitting in one of the many trains as an actual and not just imaginary traveler, experiencing journeys that last entire days and nights. Landscapes fly past the window like movable stage sets at the theater being spun around on the revolving stage. If agreeable company is present, conversation ensues, and if not, one feels a bit vexed and proceeds to light a cigar—to the annoyance of an all too sensitive fellow traveler—and produces great quantities of smoke. Or else one has a book and would like to read a bit of it, but one cannot quite, until in the end one can. The rectangle of window keeps displaying fresh new images. You watch vineyard-covered hillsides slowly falling away, houses sinking down, trees suddenly shooting up out of the earth. Clouds and meadows alternate amicably, meaningfully. "Might you give me a light from your fire there?" someone accosts you, but given your good breeding you willingly tolerate this interruption and reply "Why, of course!," and with pleasure distribute some of the superfluous embers. What a flying, rattling, rustling. Entire towns and villages are left behind on both sides as though they were lifeless images, and yet in these places human beings respire, horses whinny, a metalworker hammers away, a factory spins its wheel, a steer bellows, a child is crying, a person is consumed by bitter despair, two lovers secretly rejoice, boys are heading off to school, a midday meal is cooked in someone's kitchen, a pair of unfortunate invalids lie in bed, or two men exchange blows in some wretched altercation. But the railway keeps on flying down its precisely predetermined, prearranged path and lets all the rest of human life and activity be human life and activity. At each tidy station, people get out and in, those getting out are generally received by a mother, father, brother, son, or daughter, or else by acquaintances, and those who get in nicely say "Good day" or "Good evening," depending on where, for example, the hour hand has gotten to. And then the journey continues, crossing plains, passing by thick fir forests and splendid little garden-encircled huts for the level-crossing attendants, then passing a woodcutter on the shore of a brightly glittering lake. What lake is that, people are asking in the car. Onward. Many sit silently in their seats, surrendering to a melancholy thought or memory, a few laugh and jest, most are now eating something they have extracted from paper wrappers and boxes, and one or the other takes railway-car friendliness to the point of offering his neighbor something to eat with the calmest demeanor in the world. Thank you! But no one is even expecting to be thanked. Traveling inspires camaraderie. And how marvelous it is to ride the train in winter! Snow everywhere, snow-covered rooftops, villages, people, fields, and forests; on rainy days: dampness everywhere, fog and darkly veiled views; in the sunny springtime: blue, green, and yellow everywhere, and white blossoms. The meadows are yellow and green, sweet sunlight shimmers through the beech forest, high up in the blue sky float the gayest, whitest clouds, and in the gardens and fields there is such a blossoming, humming, and splendor that one is tempted at every station to get out and lose oneself in all this warmth, color, and beauty. And in the fall, and in the middle of summery, languid, humid high season, and again in the frosty clear winter—no, one shouldn't be so cocky as to try to cram all of this into the brief space of a newspaper article.

Nowadays anywhere there is nature, trains are also found. Soon there will no longer be a single colossus of a mountain that people have not yet begun to pierce for the sake of transport, civilization, and pleasure. There is no shortage of cable cars, and all of this is good, for it sets hands and minds in beneficial motion. To be sure, traveling by train for pleasure or business can also be quite perilous, as recent accidents have taught us; bridges can collapse, tracks can suddenly jut up in a fury and fling the train about, two trains can, owing perhaps to an oversight on the part of a single responsible official in the middle of a forest where no human habitations can be found far and wide, crash into each other—what horrific things! Or a fire can suddenly break out within a flying train, or else the train can—in holy Russia for example—be attacked by bandits. These are things that, it appears to me, display a blanched, solemn visage, but at least occurrences of this sort are met with only very rarely. Mankind cannot, after all, abandon something so *advantageous* just because of certain dangers, and the steam locomotive with all the cars hanging on behind does represent an unmistakable advantage. Many a person has already been liberated from torments, worries, and annoyances by his peaceful journey in a quiet compartment, using the railway to put his pressing plans and thoughts more or less in order in the course of long, possibly nocturnal journeys. Here the foolishnesses and pettinesses of quotidian life fall silent, triumph as they may in their usual milieu. Today one can rest while completing a journey. But one can also easily experience the most tender *adventures*, above all on express trains. How? This is something every person must discover on his own. I now come to a close, looking forward to the train trip I shall soon be making. To be honest, I don't travel much, and this is why the thought of travel fills me with such longing.

1907

WHAT BECAME OF ME

I AM, BY birth, a child of my country, by trade I am poor, my social status is that of human being, my character that of a young man, and by profession I am the author of the present autobiographical sketch. My upbringing went like this: From time to time my beloved Papa sent me out to Ridau. Ridau is a charming, ancient little town with only a single street—though a nice wide one to be sure—and a towering Gothic castle.

Ridau is home to Herr Baumgartner. I would go running off to Ridau so as swiftly to pass on to Herr Baumgartner Papa's greetings and best regards. Such was my upbringing.

My schooling and education took the form of attending a *Progymnasium* or junior high school. The *Progymnasium* is a classical seat of learning, for it was established under Napoleon the Great and First, or at least under his influence. After this, harsh Life flung me upon the path of a practicing feuilletonist. Oh, if only I had never written a feuilleton.

But Fate, which remains perpetually inscrutable, willed it thus, and would appear to have made of me a perfumed and mincing know-it-all and write-it-all, and all the oh so precious innermost cores of my being that pluck at the heartstrings of my patriotic sentiment have had—as I lament with weeping eyes and deep within my hollowed-out soul—to go by the wayside. What a cruel fate I am bound to!

And yet everything can take a turn for the better, and naïve rusticality will perhaps, who knows, return to me someday, and then I shall once more be allowed to wring my hands in isolation. For the time being, however, I appear to be sunk deep in the Gomorrah of simpering, capering correspondenthood, and very little hope persists—possibly none at all—that I shall ever again in all my days be capable of emitting a yodel such as, for example, the literarily so enterprising and worldly Ernst Zahn lets rip in so splendid and earthy a manner. Ernst Zahn and other equally shrewd individuals are champions at underscoring that they love their homeland.

Such manufacture has always eluded me. The world is wide, and human beings are a mystery, and Napoleon was a great man, and Ridau is a delightful little town, and the core of a human being never goes entirely by the wayside. What silly bigotry, these Old Auntie gossipings from the South. Berlin is such a lovely city, and its inhabitants are such hardworking, upright, and courteous human beings.

1912

FOOD FOR THOUGHT

HOW UNCERTAIN, how difficult people make one another's lives! How they belittle each other and are at pains to suspect and dishonor. How everything takes place merely for the sake of triumph. When they leave things undone, this occurs because of external exigencies, and when they err, it is never they who are at fault. Their fellow men always appear to them as obstacles, while their own person is always the highest and most noble of creatures. What efforts people make to disguise themselves with the intention of causing harm. How often we long for open, honest rudeness. At least during a fit of rage the heart chimes in. It's strange how quick people are to dismiss one another, to invoke a scornful tone, trifling with what is most noble, precious, and meaningful. And how they never grow weary of finding fault, how it never occurs to them simply to hope there might be greatness, goodness, and honesty on earth. The notion that the earth itself is honorable is something they cannot quite grasp, obvious as it appears. Only their own trifling concerns seem to them deserving of the respect that in fact they owe the world, this majestic church. How seriously they take their own sins, and how convinced they've been throughout their adult lives that nothing more refined or heed-worthy than they can possibly exist. How they persist in worshiping something utterly undeserving of worship, the ancient golden calf, the expressionless monstrosity, how industriously they believe in the unbelievable. The stars mean nothing to them: in their opinion, stars are for children; and yet what are they themselves if not unruly children intent on doing what should not be done. How good they are at spreading fearfulness all around them, well aware that they themselves are constantly beset by dark, dull, foolish fears. How fervently they long never to do anything foolish, and yet this ignoble longing is itself the most foolish thing that can be felt under the sun. They wish to be the cleverest of people, but they're the most miserable ones imaginable. A thief has done something, he's been seduced into doing something illicit and bad—but these people have never done anything at all, neither something base and heinous nor something tenderhearted and good, and they firmly resolve never to do anything that could possibly arouse attention. Indeed, they give us something to think about.

How they misapprehend themselves in their narrow-minded conviction that they are worth more than others. Out of sheer naïveté they refer to themselves as cultivated, turning up their snub noses at one another. The poor things. If only they knew how uncultivated and unschooled pride is, how poorly brought up the one who is ruled by his own incapacity to judge himself. "Come, let's go find a quiet corner where we can experience remorse on account of all the presumptuousness and lovelessness whose influence we haven't been able to break free of." This is how a person would speak if he were sensible of the slightest cultivation. "Would you like to come? There'll be a temple standing there, a holy, invisible one. Do come. You'll see, it will give you pleasure, and will do both our hearts good!" Such or similar words would be exchanged among fellow human beings. What barbarians these are who speak of culture, of all these marvelous things, of beauty that will remain forever alien to them as long as they cannot will themselves to practice beauty. All practice and motion are so far from them. They just talk and talk and talk, and for just this reason sink ever deeper into the midnight of unrefinedness, for only action is refined; talk is murky and dark, as unclean as hell itself. How they squander their time and the light, golden, fluid worth of their existence by passing hours on end in places where they exhaust their ears and minds speaking about things that a sensible, hardworking person would give a swift thought to, soon reaching a conclusion. Apparently by speaking they are attempting to come to terms with certain significations, but in this they will never succeed. No, they don't even wish to succeed, they understand perfectly well that they are indulging in a sort of linguistic gourmandizing. They're just gluttons. But gluttony cannot be anything other than an abomination; a sin committed against one's parents and children; an injustice against every other living being; an atrocity against oneself. The nights, the holy temples of life, how unspeakably they are devalued, dishonored, and desecrated by lines such as this: "Come with me, let's dash over to such-and-such a place!" The cultivated person is constantly having to dash somewhere or other, and why? This is something he himself honestly doesn't know. How ceaselessly they chase after pleasures even a blackamoor would disdain, hungering after diversions that would make even a Kalmuck shrug her shoulders in unimaginable scorn. What indignation they display when confronted with the outrageous expectation that they might calmly observe the wending of the weeks, quietly perform devotions of a sensible, lovely sort or, quite simply, go to church. Oh, by God—the Invincible One—church can make a person forget the horrors he has on his conscience and entice him to submit. Enough of all the emptinesses, loathsomenesses, soul- and heartlessnesses brought about by this garrulous modernity.

And how they suffer. You have to have lived among them, you have to have partaken in the follies they pay homage to, whose charms have been plucked bare and are no longer able to invigorate either the mind or the senses, in order to understand how they suffer. Their consolation is that it is they who set the tone in the world. What a consolation. Their pride is that they are mentioned in the press. What a thing to be proud of. Their triumph is to stand at the forefront of what people love to call progress. What an accomplishment. And beside them one sees these weary, withered, half-alive men, these soulful women whose entire souls have been eaten up and destroyed by furious, hopeless, half-mad dissatisfactions. Unfortunate women poised at the pinnacle of culture, where they dally; unenviable men; impoverished human beings. And they half admit they are impoverished. But how did they get so poor? They are dear human beings. Yes, truly. But why is it they in particular who are so unreliable, so out of sorts, withered, and querulous? This too might give us something to think about.

Spirits and gods no longer speak to them. Their lives are based solely upon sensual pleasures and trinkets when they should be founded upon reason and solid thought. They want to take striving as their basis, but this empty ascent from step to step is not a just, honorable foundation and ground. This striving would have to be conjoined in a forward-thinking way with valor and nobility, but this is not at all the case, in fact the opposite is true: schism, disintegration, unraveling. High above, nothing remains. The upper regions have been strangely depleted of development. There's no making headway, and so we are obliged to turn back—which in and of itself is something to think about.

1910

LOOKING BACK

REMEMBERING *THE TALES*
OF HOFFMANN

I WAS LIVING in the tranquillity of rural, provincial isolation, in the flat countryside where fields and forests lie about motionless and mute, the plains and plots of land appear endless, broad wide regions often prove to be only narrow strips, and vast estates slumber peacefully one beside the other.

Brown, yellow, red autumnal foliage, fog that mysteriously wrapped the wintry earth in veils; large, wet, fat snowflakes tumbling down into a morning-dark courtyard, a white park covered in snow, a winter village with village lads and village women and geese in the village street—all this I had seen.

I'd seen a poor, sick, unhappy day laborer forgotten by all the world, lying in her squalid bed of sufferings; I heard her sighs.

Forests, hills, plains silent and wordless in the dull hush of the gleaming winter sun. Here and there a solitary person, an insignificant little word, an isolated sound.

One day I left all this remoteness and all this silence behind and set off for the seductive gleam of the capital, where soon thereafter I saw *The Tales of Hoffmann* at the Komische Oper.

I felt like an astonished hayseed amid all that gleaming intoxication, the graceful, sense-beguiling tumultuousness and the blindingly elegant society gathered there.

But when the interior of the grand edifice became as silent as a tiny chamber filled with reveries and fancies of the soul, as the might and art of sound opened their divine mouths and began to sing, ring out, and resound, beginning with the overture that wheedled its way into all our souls with its bright and dark, gay and earnest melodies, only to entwine them—now constricting, now liberating from constriction—with heavenly bliss, and then soft warm song burst from the lips of the singers and songstresses, images brimming with delicate, noble, magical colors and magical figures lightly and gaily emerged to delight the eye and taste, music and painting most beautifully took possession of every heart, eye, and ear, and everything became suddenly quiet as a mouse, only to resound once more as if it wished never to stop so beautifully resounding and conquering its listeners with its desired, delightful force: pain and sounds of joy mirroring the adventure of existence, exemplifying the meaning of life, and soaring up and down the scales like angelic figures ascending and descending Jacob's ladder . . .

Oh, everything was so regally beautiful and luxurious all about our tear-filled, feverish eyes and in our hearts. All of life could now cease outright or else begin utterly anew.

What a presence to partake of! Thousands of hours flowed together to form this one single hour. Yes, what a beautiful, good, meaningful evening this was.

1916

THE TANNERS

THE INTOXICATING gleam of the dark, metropolitan streets, the lights, the people, my brother. I myself, living in my brother's apartment. I shall never forget this simple two-bedroom dwelling. It always seemed to me as if this apartment contained a sky complete with stars, moon, and clouds. Marvelous romanticism, dulcet forebodings! My brother would spend half the night at the theater, where he was making the stage sets. At three or four in the morning he would come home, and I would still be sitting there, enchanted by all the thoughts, all the lovely images wafting through my head; it was as if I no longer required sleep, as if thinking, writing, and waking were my lovely, restorative sleep, as if writing for hours and hours at my desk comprised my world, my pleasure, relaxation and peace. The dark-colored desk, so antiquated it might have been an old magician. When I pulled open its delicately worked small drawers, I imagined that sentences, words, and maxims would come leaping out. The snow-white curtains, the singing gaslight, the elongated dark room, the cat and all the becalmed waves of the long nights filled with thoughts. From time to time I would go visit the merry maids down at the girls' tavern, that was also part of it. To speak of the cat once more: she always sat on the pages filled with writing that I had laid to one side and would blink at me with her unfathomable golden eyes so strangely, with such a questioning look. Her presence was like the presence of an odd, silent fairy. Perhaps I owe this dear, silent animal a great deal. How can one know? The further I progressed in my writing, the more I felt as if I were being watched over and protected by a kindly entity. A soft, delicate large veil floated about me. But at this juncture I should also mention the liqueur that stood upon the sideboard. I partook of it as freely as I was permitted and able. Everything all around me had a soothing, invigorating influence. Certain states, circumstances, and circles are there only once, never again to appear, or else only when one is least expecting it. Are not expectations and presuppositions unholy, impertinent, and indelicate? The poet must ramble and rove, he must courageously lose himself, must always venture everything he owns, and he has to hope, or rather he is permitted: permitted to hope. —I recall that I began writing the book with a hopeless flutter of words, with all sorts of mindless sketchings and scribblings. —I never dreamed I might be capable of completing something serious, beautiful, and good. —Better ideas and, along with them, the courage to create arrived only gradually, but also all the more mysteriously, rising out of chasms of self-contempt and flippant disbelief. —It was like the morning sun rising up in the sky. Evening and morning, past and future and the so delightful present seemed to lie at my feet; before me the countryside quickened with life, and I felt as though I could grasp human activity, all of human life in my hands, that's how vividly I saw it. —One image gave way to another, and the thoughts that occurred to me played with one another like happy, graceful, well-mannered children. Filled with rapture, I clung to my joyful main idea, and as I industriously went on writing more and more, its context came into view.

1914

THE SECRETARY

I HAD THE audacity to write a book that caused quite a stir. As a consequence I was permitted to interact in a casual manner with people of substance. The doors of serious, elegant households were flung wide open to admit me, which was most certainly to my advantage. All I had to do was stroll right in and take care to behave in an agreeable manner as consistently as possible. Once I set foot in a gathering of at least forty full-blooded celebrities. Just imagine how glorious that was!

The commercial head of an association for practitioners of the fine arts one day invited me, after appropriate deliberation, to become his secretary. "I hope," he said, "that you will prove just as capable of selling pictures as you are of publishing books!" The offer was too kind to be dismissed out of hand. Accepting this proposal, I resolved that from this moment on I would consider myself fairly remarkable. I felt obliged to remind myself that a person who, upon receiving support, neither feels gratified nor shows his pleasure and gives voice to his satisfaction insults the world at large.

It's plain to see: a keen mind, superior intelligence, a high or the highest level of education and culture should, if this is somehow conceivable, be expected of all secretaries. Even their external appearance must, it goes without saying, be proper and distinguished. One assumes them to be pliant and at the same time clever, suave, gallant and at the same time in every way resolved to achieve commercial success. Elegant manners and glossy social savoir faire number decisively among their inborn qualities.

I don't know whether I did in fact display all the above-mentioned traits, but I do know that half the city came traipsing through my office. Persons of all dispositions, of every rank and station came barging more or less vigorously into the ministry, I mean headquarters: the cream of society, elegant agents, poor journeymen, sly Gypsies, unruly poets, alarmingly refined ladies, dour princes, strikingly handsome young officers, authors, actresses, sculptors, diplomats, politicians, critics, journalists, theater directors, virtuosos, celebrated scholars, publishers, and wizards in the field of finance. In and out went some who had long since arrived at the top, some who were still groping about the bottom, and others hoping to ascend—both radiantly luminous and somber, gloomy individuals. As in an odd masquerade there entered: young and old, poor and wealthy, healthy and frail, lofty and lowly, merry and morose, happy and unhappy, saucy and shy, cheerful and sad, attractive and hideous, polite and impolite, glorious and shabby, respected and despondent, the proud and the imploring, the famous and the unknown, along with faces, gestures, and figures of all genres.

Art exhibitions are known to have as their goal the advantageous display of works of art and the attracting of buyers. The secretary plays the role of intermediary or go-between, facilitating communication between artists and their extensive, art-infatuated public. It is his task to ensure that a goodly number of bargains are definitively struck, that pictures are industriously sent out the door to buyers. Persons expressing interest in these works might appear on the scene only to swiftly vanish from sight again, unfortunately for good. The secretary must be attentive, as the most unimposing man can unexpectedly prove to be a connoisseur and buyer.

For a time I imagined myself to be exceedingly skillful at the art trade. Unquestionably I was splendidly suited to taking leisurely hackney-cab rides upon pleasantly lively, bright, glittering streets and to spending half and whole hours merrily chatting with jolly artists' wives. Spirited evenings at the club regularly showed me in top form. I was a master at passing about platters heaped with delicacies, and was a frequent and enthusiastic visitor to and encourager of female painters. In such and similar respects, I acquitted myself gloriously. After the fact, however, I reached the conclusion that I cannot have been a particularly valuable, clever, prudent, and successful secretary for paintings. Specialists in the field were on several occasions seen to shrug their shoulders at the extent of my accomplishments. The head of the firm seemed to find it appealing to speak with his functionary above all on the subject of poetry and the like.

A stately successor soon reduced me to a predecessor and provided me with an occasion to lay down my post, resign my position, delicately make way, and charmingly busy myself elsewhere. Thinking poorly of me or feeling resentful because he had made so bold as to presume talents in me that I did not in fact possess was something that would never have occurred to my benefactor. To demonstrate that he was still of a mind to remain well-disposed toward me, he invited me, with a turn of phrase both courteous and jovial, to join him for supper.

1917

FRAU BÄHNI

"COME with me, we'll go visit Frau Bähni," the potentate Bösiger said to me. At the time I was something resembling Bösiger's favored protégé. He no doubt found it agreeable to consort with me because I was inexperienced. My innocuousness gave him a sort of pleasure, and the infelicities I now and then displayed made him laugh. It's well known that powerful, influential gentlemen like to spend time in the company of people who have no importance at all. In those days, I was playing the role of youthful novice in the circles that set the tone, i.e., the world of culture, intellect, and elegance. I would turn up here and there, advantageously or not, and was collecting my first experiences of society. In the salons, by the way, as I soon discovered, I had not the slightest success, and perhaps it was precisely this circumstance that secured me Bösiger's favor. It was impossible for him to see me as a rival. Later, though, he reconsidered his view of me, and in time he began to be taken aback by my behavior, and that was the end of his patronage.

We got into a hackney cab and together rode through the densely populated streets of the capital to the home of beautiful Frau Bähni, who lived in the most elegant, posh, desirable part of town. She was at home and received us most courteously. It was three in the afternoon, a rainy day. Much of what I have experienced in the wide world has vanished completely from my head over the years, but I still vividly recall Frau Bähni, and the afternoon hour I am describing here impressed itself on me and remains an indelible memory. Frau Bähni's husband maintained extremely close business ties to capitalist Bösiger. She herself was strikingly beautiful. Her appearance and person always produced a stir, and she laid claim to a certain renown as a figure worthy of admiration. She held and retained this fame for a relatively long time. As for her apartment, I must confess that I've never seen a prettier abode. Frau Bähni greeted us with the most courteous and endearing smile, and her beautiful, majestic face seemed to express the most vibrant joy.

She pressed our hands in turn and then with what appeared to be the greatest amiability invited us to enter the parlor. Bösiger, by the way, had always assured me that Frau Bähni was an enigma. "She's frightfully clever, and yet I don't fully believe in her cleverness," he'd said. Bösiger had a reputation for being both a witty and a domineering, violent person. There was a time when people compared him to Napoleon. His boldly enterprising nature and his ruthless drive were legendary. When he entered the home of Frau Bähni, whose beauty he was forced to acknowledge and who seemed to make a deep impression on him, it was with the expression of a person tormented by all sorts of spleen. He appeared to be a bit awkward and self-conscious and to be aggrieved at this circumstance. Frau Bähni sat down at the piano and began to play, and I had the strange impression that she was playing music primarily because she felt a need to calm her nerves. A conversation had not yet arisen. The two of us, or perhaps all three, feigned a sense of comfort that in truth was nonexistent and a pleasure none of us felt. Bösiger wrinkled his forehead. Frau Bähni interrupted her playing and with defiant coldness in her large, beautiful eyes approached her adversary. I began to realize that the two of them had been preparing for this hostile encounter for quite some time, and I was extremely curious to hear the words that would be uttered by these two persons who now stood facing each other like two adversaries on the field of battle. Something like a drama was beginning to unfold. I took a good look at Bösiger, who sat there stiffly, and I could see quite clearly by the various small signs he was giving that he found himself in a state of extreme agitation. The elegant, cold smile he saw fit to place upon his lips was askew. At this moment he was almost ugly. His clever, interesting face that was usually almost handsome was contorted and pale. Apparently he was fighting an exceptionally difficult internal battle. People who are spoiled suffer terribly when their self-love is dealt a blow. Frau Bähni clearly had the advantage over him, and this appeared to be something that Bösiger could under no circumstances tolerate.

"I love you," he said in a constrained, forced voice. "I don't wish to hear anything of the sort," she replied. "You are the most beautiful woman in the world, and I worship you," he said. "Please do stop," she unsparingly countered. She gazed at him directly, penetratingly, all merciless distrust. It was clear that she did not attribute to Bösiger's words even the slightest credibility, or else she was being political and found it appropriate to feign disbelief. "Here the veil is being lifted on a daredevil liaison," I whispered to myself, at pains to be as quiet as a mouse. "So you refuse to be friendly to me. You thrust me away. You slice my fondest hopes to ribbons, and it means nothing to you to trample on my heart. Warmth leaves you cold, and on friendship you place no value. You are treating me with intentional frostiness, heartlessly rejecting all closeness and familiarity. Faced with the tenderness I feel for you, you do not bat an eyelash. Either you are indifferent or you are obstinately making a show of indifference. You are tormenting, martyring me, and it gives you pleasure to see me so distraught. This is not good, and I would like to know how I have merited such unfriendliness." —To this outpouring of openness from a man whom she would not previously have thought capable of candor, her only response was: "It is inappropriate for you to speak in this way." The capitalist and man of influence was trembling with fury. In fact he had not yet been the least bit candid. I sensed this, but at the same time I sensed that Frau Bähni had not yet spoken candidly either. No one speaks the truth here, in these circles that set the tone for society at large. —Perhaps a word of truth is out of the question, if only because people here are too clever and are acquainted with thousands of truths and untruths. The knowledge of human nature is too rich, the treasury of experiences in fact already too replete. In a sense, speaking the truth presupposes a certain narrow-mindedness.

"You know," Bösiger said, rising from his chair, "that I can bring harm to your husband and therefore also, of course, to yourself, and can do so in such a way that no one will be in a position—a position I would find unfortunate—to accuse me of ignoble intentions. There are means and ways, my lady, to make things quite unpleasant for your husband. The power to force you to hear my suit and attach to my assurances the belief and importance they require is within my grasp. Your and your husband's interests and therefore also your prudence must surely counsel you not to breech this friendship." This language was quite clearly being dictated by ardent hatred, for Bösiger was generally a man of good taste and culture. He was visibly made to suffer by what his passion was forcing him to say. Frau Bähni's breast heaved tempestuously, she held her hand to her violently pounding heart yet maintained a flawless composure and with admirable serenity responded as follows: "Herr Bösiger, you go too far. Certainly you can cause dire harm to my poor husband, I am quite aware of this, but I also know that I have the lovely right to suppose that we shall have the strength to endure the consequences of your revenge. And I hardly think that your revenge, regardless of how methodically you engineer it, will succeed in entirely destroying my husband and me. I am not afraid of you and what you will do, for I assume that all of us without exception are, in the end, frail human beings, for which reason I am inclined to presume that there are limits to your power and your importance. You will comport yourself as you see fit, and you will always be a welcome guest here as soon as you display the sort of civilized behavior customary when associating with women who enjoy a certain status in society. I hope that by tomorrow morning you yourself will despise these threats you have uttered."

A bell rang outside, and a moment later Herr Bähni entered. Courteous greetings were exchanged as if nothing at all had transpired. Bösiger rose to the occasion with an utterly astonishing display of ingenuousness and conviviality. He demonstrated talent in the truest sense and proved to be the most splendid confabulator. I felt sincere admiration for him. He was utterly in control and also showed himself in the best light. He sparkled with witticisms, and Frau Bähni found herself compelled to listen to everything he said with the utmost curiosity.

1916

FULL

SO MANY times, as I rode through the streets and hubbub of Berlin in the quaint, lumbering, and yet buoyantly plodding horse-drawn omnibus, which never failed to invigorate and charm me anew, I would hear the aging, good-natured conductor humbly and humorously uttering a single insignificant and yet also at that moment quite significant word, which in addition, by the way, was written for the sake of correctness and order upon a panel that could be either concealed or displayed. When the inscription

FULL

was hanging tidily and properly in its place, people knew that for the time being no one else would be allowed to climb and clamber aboard because the gondola or pleasure palace rolling along on its wheels was already packed suffocatingly full, a regrettable circumstance that was announced in no uncertain terms by the warning placard: "Stop! Whosoever they may be, this line they shall not cross!" At times, however, despite the rejecting, dismissive plaque, there would be a crowd pressing forward, expressing the impetuous desire to climb up and be carried off. And then someone, such as the chamberlain on duty, would say in a courteous voice, "Folks, we're full up," or he would say, "No shoving, please. It won't do any good," or perhaps it would occur to him to say, "With the greatest pleasure, ladies and gentlemen, would I invite you to climb aboard and take your seats, but it is my harsh duty to draw your attention to the fact that the car is already stuffed to the cracks with passengers. I do beg your pardon for having to deny you access and entry." Sallies and attacks on one side, rebuffs and refusals on the other, the vessel continues to sail calmly and gaily through all the metropolitan traffic, which almost resembles an ocean. Once again some hasty hothead is about to leap aboard, and once again an imperturbable "Full!" resounds in the daredevil's ears, whereupon he is obliged to circumspectly remove his foot from the footboard once more.

Once when the omnibus was cruising full steam ahead, everything proceeding smoothly and properly, and with no one even remotely plotting an ambush or violent coup, someone slipped aboard —a person who apparently had been accustomed from an early age to go through thick and thin and strike down anyone and anything that got in his way.

"Full up, sir," the official remarked.

"Stupid, ridiculous nonsense," replied Monsieur Dreadnought. He was without a doubt the sort of person who thought it advisable to engage in the most ruthless power politics. "I beg your pardon, did you not hear what I said?" the good carman inquired. But now a veritable downpour of invectives was unleashed upon his unfortunate head. This powerful flood of unforeseen unpleasantnesses was so overwhelming that the good man was forced to give in. All the same he complained, saying:

"It's just not right, not right at all, and it's a good thing not all people are like this gentleman who's cursing me even though all I did was tell him we were full. It was my duty to tell him so, but certain people insist on trampling and flattening everything once they've made up their minds to do something. I don't go around saying 'full' for my own amusement, or because I want to antagonize people, or out of Schadenfreude. Every person has his tasks to perform and his duties to fulfill, and it just happens to be my duty to tell people 'full' when the car is full up. It isn't fair for a person to take offense like that. It's downright preposterous how quick some people are to fly into a rage. Well then! I'll stick with the ones who have some sense; thanks and praises be to God, there are still some of them left."

This is what the conductor said as the omnibus unhurriedly trundled on its way.

1916

HORSE AND WOMAN

LET ME not forget to write down two small memories from my stay in the metropolis. One concerns a horse's head, the other an old, poor match-seller. Both these things, the horse and the woman, are surrounded by night. One night, as on so many others that had already been frittered away and poured out into oblivion, I was roaming through the streets in my elegant, though admittedly only borrowed overcoat, when at one of the busiest spots I beheld a horse harnessed to a heavy cart. The horse was standing there quietly in the indefinite darkness, and many, many people were hurrying by, passing the beautiful animal without paying it even the slightest heed. I too was hurrying past, I was in a big rush. A person whose ambition it is to go in search of amusement is always in a terrible hurry. But struck by the marvelous sight of the white horse standing in the black night, I stopped in my tracks. The long strands of hair hung down to the animal's large eyes from which a nameless sorrow peered out. The horse stood there unmoving, as if it were a white, ghostly vision just arisen from the grave, displaying a humility and patience that spoke of majesty. But I was drawn on; after all, I was in search of amusement. Another night, too, found me out and about in pursuit of the most wretched entertainment. I had already passed through all sorts of public houses when I turned onto an unlit street, and then a shout came to me from the darkness: "Matches, young sir!" It was an old, poor woman who had cried out thus. I stopped short, for I happened to be filled with heartfelt good spirits, reached into my vest pocket to find a coin and gave it to the woman without taking any of her wares. How she thanked me then and wished me good fortune in the dark future. And how she held out her old, cold, gaunt hand to me! I took her hand and pressed it, and then, happy at this small experience, continued on my way.

1914

FRAU WILKE

ONE DAY, when I was looking for a suitable room, I entered a curious house just outside the city and close to the city tramway, an elegant, oldish, and seemingly rather neglected house, whose exterior had a singularity which at once captivated me.

On the staircase, which I slowly mounted, and which was wide and bright, were smells and sounds as of bygone elegance.

What they call former beauty is extraordinarily attractive to some people. Ruins are rather touching. Before the residues of noble things our pensive, sensitive inward selves involuntarily bow. The remnants of what was once distinguished, refined, and brilliant infuse us with compassion, but simultaneously also with respect. Bygone days and old decrepitude, how enchanting you are!

On the door I read the name "Frau Wilke."

Here I gently and cautiously rang the bell. But when I realized that it was no use ringing, since nobody answered, I knocked, and then somebody approached.

Very guardedly and very slowly somebody opened the door. A gaunt, thin, tall woman stood before me, and asked in a low voice: "What is it you want?"

Her voice had a curiously dry and hoarse sound.

"May I see the room?"

"Yes, of course. Please come in."

The woman led me down a strangely dark corridor to the room, whose appearance immediately charmed and delighted me. Its shape was, as it were, refined and noble, a little narrow perhaps, yet proportionately tall. Not without a sort of irresolution, I asked the price, which was extremely moderate, so I took the room without more ado.

It made me glad to have done this, for a strange state of mind had much afflicted me for some time past, so I was unusually tired and longed to rest. Weary of all groping endeavor, depressed and out of sorts as I was, any acceptable security would have satisfied me, and the peace of a small resting place could not have been other than wholly welcome.

"What are you?" the lady asked.

"A poet!" I replied.

She went away without a word.

An earl, I think, might live here, I said to myself as I carefully examined my new home. This charming room, I said, proceeding with my soliloquy, unquestionably possesses a great advantage: it is very remote. It's quiet as a cavern here. Definitely: here I really feel I am concealed. My inmost want seems to have been gratified. The room, as I see it, or think I see it, is, so to speak, half dark. Dark brightness and bright darkness are floating everywhere. That is most commendable. Let's look around! Please don't put yourself out, sir! There's no hurry at all. Take just as much time as you like. The wall-paper seems, in parts, to be hanging in sad, mournful shreds from the wall. So it is! But that is precisely what pleases me, for I do like a certain degree of raggedness and neglect. The shreds can go on hanging; I'll not let them be removed at any price, for I am completely satisfied with them being there. I am much inclined to believe that a baron once lived here. Officers perhaps drank champagne here. The curtain by the window is tall and slender, it looks old and dusty; but being so prettily draped, it betokens good taste and reveals a delicate sensibility. Outside in the garden, close to the window, stands a birch tree. Here in summer the green will come laughing into the room, on the dear gentle branches all sorts of singing birds will gather, for their delight as well as for mine. This distinguished old writing table is wonderful, handed surely down from a past age of subtle feeling. Probably I shall write essays at it, sketches, studies, little stories, or even long stories, and send these, with urgent requests for quick and friendly publication, to all sorts of stern and highly reputable editors of papers and periodicals like, for example, *The Peking Daily News*, or *Mercure de France*, whence, for sure, prosperity and success must come.

The bed seems to be all right. In this case I will and must dispense with painstaking scrutiny. Then I saw, and here remark, a truly strange and ghostly hatstand, and the mirror there over the basin will tell me faithfully every day how I look. I hope the image it will give me to see will always be a flattering one. The couch is old, consequently pleasant and appropriate. New furniture easily disturbs one, because novelty is always importunate, always obstructs us. A Dutch and a Swiss landscape hang, as I observe to my glad satisfaction, modestly on the wall. Without a doubt, I shall look time and again at these two pictures most attentively. Regarding the air in this chamber, I would nevertheless deem it credible, or rather postulate at once with certitude almost, that for some time here no thought has been given to regular and, it seems, wholly requisite ventilation. I do declare that there is a smell of decay about the place. To inhale stale air provides a certain peculiar pleasure. In any case, I can leave the window open for days and weeks on end; then the right and good will stream into the room.

"You must get up earlier. I cannot allow you to stay in bed so long," Frau Wilke said to me. Beyond this, she did not say much.

This was because I spent entire days lying in bed.

I was in a bad way. Decrepitude surrounded me. I lay there as if in heaviness of heart; I neither knew nor could find myself anymore. All my once lucid and gay thoughts floated in obscure confusion and disarray. My mind lay as if broken in fragments before my grieving eyes. The world of thought and of feeling was jumbled and chaotic. Everything dead, empty, and hopeless to the heart. No soul, no joy anymore, and only faintly could I remember that there were times when I was happy and brave, kind and confident, full of faith and joy. The pity of it all! Before and behind me, and all around me, not the slightest prospect anymore.

Yet I promised Frau Wilke to get up earlier, and in fact I did then also begin to work hard.

Often I walked in the neighboring forest of fir and pine, whose beauties, wonderful winter solitudes, seemed to protect me from the onset of despair. Ineffably kind voices spoke down to me from the trees: "You must not come to the dark conclusion that everything in the world is hard, false, and wicked. But come often to us; the forest likes you. In its company you will find health and good spirits again, and entertain more lofty and beautiful thoughts."

Into society, that is, where the big world forgathers, I never went. I had no business there, because I had no success. People who have no success with people have no business with people.

Poor Frau Wilke, soon afterwards you died.

Whoever has been poor and lonely himself understands other poor and lonely people all the better. At least we should learn to understand our fellow beings, for we are powerless to stop their misery, their ignominy, their suffering, their weakness, and their death.

One day Frau Wilke whispered, as she stretched out her hand and arm to me: "Hold my hand. It's like ice."

I took her poor, old, thin hand in mine. It was cold as ice.

Frau Wilke crept about her home now like a ghost. Nobody visited her. For days she sat alone in her unheated room.

To be alone: icy, iron terror, foretaste of the grave, forerunner of unpitying death. Oh, whoever has been himself alone can never find another's loneliness strange.

I began to realize that Frau Wilke had nothing to eat. The lady who owned the house, and later took Frau Wilke's rooms, allowing me to stay in mine, brought, of course in pity for her forsaken state, every midday and evening a cup of broth, but not for long, and so Frau Wilke faded away. She lay there, no longer moving: and soon she was taken to the city hospital, where, after three days, she died.

One afternoon soon after her death, I entered her empty room, into which the good evening sun was shining, gladdening it with rose-bright, gay and soft colors. There I saw on the bed the things which the poor lady had till recently worn, her dress, her hat, her sunshade, and her umbrella, and, on the floor, her small delicate boots. The strange sight of them made me unspeakably sad, and my peculiar state of mind made it seem to me almost that I had died myself, and life in all its fullness, which had often appeared so huge and beautiful, was thin and poor to the point of breaking. All things past, all things vanishing away, were more close to me than ever. For a long time I looked at Frau Wilke's possessions, which now had lost their mistress and lost all purpose, and at the golden room, glorified by the smile of the evening sun, while I stood there motionless, not understanding anything anymore.

Yet, after standing there dumbly for a time, I was gratified and grew calm. Life took me by the shoulder and its wonderful gaze rested on mine. The world was as living as ever and beautiful as at the most beautiful times. I quietly left the room and went out into the street.

1915
Translated by Christopher Middleton

FRAU SCHEER

MY KNOWLEDGE of this woman's life remains sketchy. Frau Scheer was out of the ordinary, and talented in the extreme. Statements she made in my presence served to indicate then as now that she had spent her youth gaily and happily in the provinces. When she spoke of her childhood, there was always an indescribable, bittersweet rapture in her gaze. Her words summoned up a pretty, tidy little town surrounded by forest, fields, and green meadows. It made her happy to be permitted to speak of these bygone days, and if it was my humble person who provided the occasion for this quiet happiness, I shall make so bold as to consider this a modest achievement on my part, as for a time there was no one old Frau Scheer saw more of than the author of these lines, who for several reasons took a pronounced interest in this eccentric, aging woman. I was the one to whom she told things, this poor, isolated female all alone in the world, I who with great pleasure lent his ear, listening attentively to her words. I was gripped by the peculiar fate of this—millionairess. Frau Scheer was a millionaire several times over. What poor creatures we human beings are, so variously deceived. This millionairess, this wealthy Frau Scheer, thanked me most touchingly and was glad when I announced my desire to come into her room in the evening and sit with her beside the lamp for a little while. Frau Scheer was ugly; the passions of a turbulent business career, sorrows, a sea of troubles and grueling worries, haste and the pursuit of commercial successes, the torments of raging jealousy and ongoing toils had imprinted upon her face the mark of the repugnant and repulsive. Nonetheless I easily succeeded in discovering in this face a beauty that had not yet been fully extinguished, and in the evening, with the yellow sheen of the lamplight streaming over her features, old Frau Scheer became oddly lovely, and the way she then spoke and sat there was both captivating and moving. As I learned just before her death from a personage who was close to her, she is supposed to have said once that she would have been able to acquire a fortune of twenty million if Heaven had given her a different husband.

I have a photograph of Frau Scheer in which she is shown as a young woman and looks utterly charming. She married a happy-go-lucky, good-natured man who wished to enjoy his days upon this earth. His wife then manifested a truly demonic talent for speculating with fortune. She arrived in the capital during the great *Gründerzeit* period of industrial expansion, and here she found ample opportunity to develop her ingenious capabilities. In no time, she and her husband became rich. The money that now flowed into the pockets of this pleasure-seeking man drove him to carry on in the most hair-raising fashion. He surrounded himself with friends and pursued a dissolute lifestyle. He was a simple, good, innocuous man for whom the purpose of these riches was to squander them. This is much the way Asian and African princes comport themselves when they arrive in European cities. There are two sorts of people in the world: those who expend money on sensual debaucheries, and those who have a peculiar love of money and therefore manage it in the most faithful, cautious way. Frau Scheer was born to manage funds, while her husband was born to waste and squander them. Some cannot seem to value money, while others fail to value pleasure—and the life Scheer was leading verged on the monstrous. When it was getting on to evening, he would fill all his pockets with hundred- and thousand-mark banknotes, and thus excellently equipped he would betake himself off, as one says, and when this man—who was easily made drunk—had been plundered by dissolute women, villainous waiters, and other sorts of robbers and knaves, they would deposit him in a hackney cab to be driven slumberously home, and when his wife, this indefatigable business-woman, saw her husband arriving in this state, docking wretchedly in the harbor of their marriage, in full knowledge of the fact that this miserable, base junket had once again cost enormous sums, she was seized with fury at the man's cloddishness, she felt soiled and offended, and all her limbs trembled with indignation, disgust, pain, and horror.

I am in no way capable of judging whether there is any truth to the rumor that came to me shortly before Frau Scheer's death from the mouth of the aforementioned personage who numbered among her friends, a rumor that sought to convince me that my unfortunate Frau Scheer had given some thought to arranging to have her imprudent husband murdered. According to this rumor, as the mischief being wrought by this frivolous man was becoming ever more serious, Frau Scheer entered into apparently quite close relations with a strange, romantic, exalted individual, a physician, meaning to avail herself of this overwrought dreamer and visionary as what we might refer to as a willing, chivalrously eager tool, so to speak, of revenge and retribution. Certainly the aggrieved woman had great and justified cause for her honest, deeply felt wrath; certainly she herself, as I had ample opportunity to observe, possessed an easily swayed, sensitive character and was ruled by a volatile temper, and yet I did and do not believe in the above so horrific and lugubrious claim. Frau Scheer was at the same time gentle, she had a visible streak of sweet kindness, and—despite everything, and then despite everything all over again—she did love, respect, and esteem her husband. Perhaps that harebrained adventurer, that dark midnight doctor had indeed once made her a sinister offer of this sort; but she most assuredly would have rejected it, admonishing her friend—if in fact she ever had one—to behave in a proper, sensible way. I do not doubt this for a moment, although I do concede that Frau Scheer was a peculiar and, as said before, utterly out-of-the-ordinary human being. Meanwhile Scheer fell ill, and it wasn't long before he died at what was by no means an advanced age but rather, relatively speaking, the prime of life, and Frau Scheer was left alone.

From this point until her own passing, the woman who is the object of this "study" led a life that could not possibly have been spent any more miserably, restlessly, and tormentedly by any other person. No beggar woman ever had so poor, lamentable, and shabby an existence. No poor worker or worker's wife ever led such a poor, sad life of woe as did this exceedingly wealthy woman, and if ever in this world, which is a mystery and will always remain one, there lived a hero or heroine of everyday life, this Frau Scheer was a heroine. She fought an unheard-of battle and suffered and endured unheard-of adversity. A single glance into her apartment revealed everything she endured. Was Frau Scheer mad? Often when I saw her chasing about or speaking, walking, or writing in such haste, making phone calls, running about and carrying on, this admittedly somewhat bold and audacious thought did occur to me. Obstinacy often comes awfully close to madness. Frau Scheer could have built herself a palace, a wonderful summer and a winter residence and dwelt there like a baroness, countess, or princess, but the human heart is a curious thing, and the heart of our peculiar lady was devoted entirely to her business ventures, and she had no interest in all the pleasures, splendors, and beauties of the world. Frau Scheer was shockingly tightfisted; stinginess and the earning of money were like two dear sons to her—she saw in them the best and the most precious of what the world had to offer. Yes, I must confess that this woman struck me as infinitely fascinating: I sympathized with her. Sympathies are strange things; sometimes they can scarcely be explained. I found this millionairess sympathetic although she was so ugly; her sorrow and misery cast a romantic spell that made her appear beautiful.

The way I made her acquaintance is quite simple. One day I joined a bizarre household to live as the tenant of a certain Frau Wilke, who died soon thereafter. The owner of the building—in fact my Frau Scheer—sent word to me that she was happy to allow me to go on living in my room. This news was welcome, since I was virtually in love with my little chamber, which was situated in a charmingly out-of-the-way corner. And so Frau Scheer became my new landlady. At the time, my own finances were in so sorry a state they could not possibly have been any worse; as a result of this, I was quiet, moody, and withdrawn, and thus at the beginning I paid no attention at all to this in her own way highly significant woman. I sometimes saw her when I peered out my lovely window, walking up and down in the garden in bizarre, gypsylike attire, her hair disheveled, and I was honestly astonished at the sight of this carelessly clad female figure. As for the rest I took no notice of her whatever, wicked fellow that I was, even though, as it later dawned on me, the woman had no doubt wished to keep me in her apartment above all for the sake of having some human being near her. Loneliness, what a fearsome wild beast you are! But what sort of heedful attentiveness might I have bestowed on this woman at a time when I was occupied exclusively with paltry, naked thoughts of how I might possibly manage to improve my own lot even a little. In those days I myself resembled a half-starved beast of prey casting about with wildly flaming eyes for a suitable opportunity to hunt down some quarry to improve its precarious position. Venture into that savage metropolis, dear reader, and you will see for yourself how abruptly glamour and good fortune alternate there with deprivation and worry, and how people undermine each other's subsistence, as each does his best to cast down the other's successes and tread upon them so as to make success his own.

"I am poor, and I am steeling myself for even more poverty," I wrote, as I recall, to delightful Auguste, who had been my sweet little lady friend, "and you will probably never again respond to a letter containing such doleful confessions. I understand you womenfolk; you are only lovely, good, and kind to those who visibly enjoy good fortune in this world. Penury, indigence, and misfortune repulse you. Forgive the anguish that is not ashamed to write such things. What am I capable of offering you when I am scarcely able to keep my own head above water? Clearly things are over between us, no?, for you will surely find it expedient to shun me. This I can understand. And I as well am joyfully taking leave of you today, because now it is time for me to invest what strength I possess in fighting an all too unlovely struggle for survival. Oh, all those rose scenes, that divine, gay exuberance you bestowed on me, that laughter! I shall always be prepared to think back on a happiness whose mischievous originator you were. Let me kiss you once more in thought, tenderly, as if we were still entitled to dally thus. No doubt you have already begun to forget me. And so adieu forever." —I have interposed this letter in order to offer the reader a brief, elegant diversion. The letter remained unanswered, and this is what I'd expected, well-acquainted as I was with my clever little Auguste. Despite all her amusing diminutiveness, she was a soul of great resolve. She went on her way, and this pleased me. But now back to Frau Scheer. Back to the matter at hand.

Around the neighborhood, in the shops, at the grocer's or hairdresser's, on the street and on the stairs, people spoke of that stingy old witch, that "Scheer," and all too cheap and superficial phrases were invoked to condemn her. The picture of her being sketched out had nothing at all to do with reality and truth. Later on it was an easy matter for me to see through it all. Meanwhile I was gradually coming into contact and acquaintance with this so widely discussed and disparaged woman. She complained about my taciturnity and reticence, but I found it appropriate to continue to be reticent and taciturn. I realized she was utterly abandoned. Apart from a lady of quite elegant appearance who came to the house now and then, and apart from Emma, her former maid, who came every day to offer her a small amount of assistance in the household, no one ever visited. The visitors she did receive—who made their presence known with larger and smaller amounts of noise—were workmen and businessmen of all sorts; Frau Scheer was a landowner and real estate investor on a grand scale. Or else there would be a ring or a knock at the door, and tenants would uneasily enter, either coming to pay the rent that was due or bounding up to declare that they were in no position to pay. Or then I would suddenly hear shouting and hurled invectives in the hall. This would be some person who believed himself unfairly treated. And so Frau Scheer had to telephone the local police station for help, whereupon policemen appeared, and thus the dwelling of a woman who had enormous sums of money at her disposal witnessed one unlovely scene after another, countless unfortunate incidents, so that the lady and mistress of this home found it a comfort and experienced the greatest refreshment and relief when she was able to sit quietly in her room in the evening and weep, simply that: weep undisturbed.

My room and Frau Scheer's writing and living room lay side by side, and often I heard through the thin wall a sound that I was only ever able to explain to myself with the thought that someone was weeping. The tears of a wealthy, stingy woman are surely no less doleful and deplorable, and speak a surely no less sad and moving language than the tears of a poor little child, a poor woman, or a poor man; tears in the eyes of mature human beings are appalling, for they bear witness to a helplessness one might scarcely believe possible. When a child cries, this is immediately comprehensible, but when old people are induced or compelled to weep despite their advanced years, this reveals to the one hearing and seeing this the world's wretchedness and untenability, and such a person cannot escape the oppressive, devastating thought that everything—everything—that moves upon this unfortunate earth is weak, shaky, and questionable, the quarry and haphazard plaything of an insufficiency that has entwined itself about all that exists. No, it is not good when a human being still weeps at an age when one should consider it a divinely lovely activity to dry the tears of children.

With the exception of her niece, wife of the Cantonal Executive Councillor So-and-so, with whom she maintained, or so it seemed, amiable relations, Frau Scheer seemed to be on irrevocably bad terms with all her relatives. Some of them, I was later told, were her mortal enemies as a result of a vicious and deep-rooted feud. If what I heard people saying immediately following Frau Scheer's death is true— namely, that one of her sisters had been living in the most squalid circumstances without receiving any support whatever from wealthy Frau Scheer, and that she even tormented and oppressed this sister so as to mock her misery on top of everything else while remaining utterly unmoved by it—of course this information casts a peculiar light on this friend of mine, and I am wondering with some degree of urgency whether she truly was capable of such dastardly, merciless conduct. Her relatives seemed to have the worst possible opinion of her. To be sure, one mustn't underestimate the role played in this by personal animosity. They tried to present Frau Scheer to me as a heinous actress whose mind was entirely filled with insatiable egotism. Hatred, distrust, wickedness, and duplicity, they averred, were the purpose and meaning of her depraved, corrupt existence. I listened to all these things without saying much in reply, but meanwhile was thinking thoughts of my own, for these people who were doing their best to make me think of the unfortunate woman in bad and bleak terms by no means struck me as being so terribly pure of heart and good themselves. At the same time it pained me that Frau Scheer no longer had even a good remembrance in this world where she had so struggled and suffered. But here I must draw attention to yet another strange circumstance, for I may not leave anything important unmentioned that might be able to give life to or illuminate my subject. In Frau Scheer's immediate neighborhood, a young, pretty girl—a real goose, by the way, the little daughter of a police inspector—was generally thought to be poised to inherit Frau Scheer's fortune. I often saw this girl at the apartment, and I have to say that this rather silly little thing of eighteen who was presumptuous enough to surround herself with all sorts of fond, happy illusions, did not make a particularly favorable impression on me. If the gullible parents of this girl indulged frivolous hopes with even more frivolous complacence, then they found themselves utterly deceived in a quite instructive way. For later on not so much as a single dotted *i* was found in favor of Little Miss Cheeky, and the hope-filled damsel inherited not a penny. This should be the fate of all those who are not ashamed to base their prospects on the death of a fellow human being.

Frau Scheer possessed a by no means unattractive if slightly stout figure. At times she displayed a quite winsome, graceful bearing. Dressed in her Sunday best, she looked every bit the grand, elegant lady. But on several occasions I saw her on the street coming back from her buildings, and each time I was shocked at her downcast, crestfallen appearance. Her weary, dragging gait said with sorrowful plainness: "I shall die soon." As she walked like this, she gazed up at the sky. One often sees women casting their eyes up to heaven in this way. Sometimes her eyes were filled with dreadful entreaties for a bit of love. When she smiled in gay spirits, there was something profoundly captivating about her. In her youth she must have been loveliness itself. She herself once smilingly confessed that as a child she'd been the family darling. On the inside, perhaps, she had remained a dreamy small-town girl. Poor little thing! Poor deceived dreamer! Frau Scheer had very delicate, tiny feet. In her kitchen, on the kitchen floor, I often saw her charming, snug little booties, which interested me greatly because they looked as if they wished to relate the life story of their mistress. The fanatical love of money that resided within her and the strange, passionate pleasure she took in acquiring it seemed to me genuine small-town idiosyncrasies. In her youngest years she had once traveled with her husband to Switzerland, and even as an old woman she spoke with the most charming enthusiasm of this country's beauties. She had seen Lucerne and ascended to the top of the Rigi. A remark she made in passing revealed that she had been a devoted cyclist. Admittedly these are trifles, but these trifles mean a great deal to me, and I am incapable of coldly passing over these trivialities. Besides which, I don't really consider anything trivial. Frau Scheer was kind enough to encourage me to walk around in her apartment without ceremony as though the apartment belonged to me, and of course I was glad to take advantage of such agreeable freedom. The apartment contained nothing else of particular note. In the woman's study, there were always piles of business papers lying about waiting to be dealt with. The kitchen was visibly unclean, the salon teeming with disorder and dust. Frau Scheer was utterly devoid of domesticity despite the fact that she owned fifteen buildings. How often she sighed. Sometimes it seemed to me when I saw her like this that I was about to witness her collapsing beneath the burden of her work.

I recall that the two of us stood one night conversing at the door to my room. It was the first time in quite a while that I had spoken with her at length in such a friendly way. She listened to me with a silent, lovely, very tender attentiveness. My loquaciousness seemed to be giving her the greatest pleasure. She too spoke. Frau Scheer always spoke with admirable lightness. "How cold, stiff, and reserved you've been," she said, "even though we've lived so long together under a single roof. That has often hurt me, but now I am all the happier to hear you speak to me in such an agreeably friendly, familiar way. You've always kept to yourself, scarcely bothering to greet or even look at me, this caused me pain. And yet, as I now see and hear, you can be so very kind. Sometimes I thought, because you once said to me that you love solitary walks and often go into the woods, that you might be contemplating doing yourself harm, or else that something unfortunate might befall you there in the forest. Fortunately, though, I see you standing before me in good health, and I am glad." "Forgive me if I've ever been discourteous," I said. She replied with obvious kindness: "It doesn't matter." She stood there with such a touchingly beautiful, youthfully fresh lightness, and I secretly reproached myself for my earlier behavior. I held out my hand to indicate to her that I did indeed value the friendliness and confidingness of this moment as something humanly beautiful, and she pressed my hand with marked pleasure. This was a peculiar hour filled with simple, strong warmth; I shall remember it forever.

Since I frequently found myself idle for lack of regular employment, while Frau Scheer was overburdened, I offered my services to her when the opportunity presented itself so that I might assist her with her many business dealings, and she did not for a moment hesitate to acquiesce to my proposal. How lovely it is, and how good it feels to lend a hand to a person in need of help. It makes me deeply happy today, when all of this lies far in the past, that I did manage, while there was still time, to set aside my indifference, coldness, and lack of sympathy and enter into a good relationship with this woman in which sympathy played an important role. It seemed to me as if this were making me much younger again. I wrote letters, ran this and that errand, received covetous and pressing visitors in Frau Scheer's absence, took delivery of payments, for which I issued receipts with my nicest and warmest thanks, prepared contracts, ran and strolled about as a delegate and private secretary, as messenger and commissioner and confidant, stopping by all sorts of institutes and buildings, a task in which my sound knowledge of the area, acquired earlier in the course of many pleasurable walks, stood me in good stead. As a punctual and trusty Scheer employee, I inspected newly constructed buildings, during which it pleased me to assume the most severe, unrelenting office and business expression when dealing with craftsmen and handymen in order to assure myself of being highly respected by people who are not so fond of showing respect; my head was filled with parcels of land, leases, mortgages, properties, and buildings, and I was the consummate surveyor, inspector, and administrator. I often found myself walking and ambling through heavily populated streets and alleyways carrying ready cash to the tune of twenty or thirty thousand, and many a cautious bank official at first hesitated a little before paying out to me these high, alarming sums, no doubt wondering how a wealthy woman could dare place such great trust in such a one as me. When I returned home, I always received a touchingly beautiful and grateful smile as a reward for my assiduous, honest, and upright services. Lord knows it's true that service of this sort always gave and gives me great and joyful pleasure.

Frau Scheer in her turn was in no way lacking in attentiveness toward me insofar as she took no rent from me at all. And so I lived there free of charge; she also took pleasure in cooking for me in her spare time. This is a matter in which, as you can imagine, I was happy to let her have her way. First off, my own affairs were, as I have already emphasized, in a sorry state, and secondly I saw with my own eyes and smelled with my nose and in general quite clearly noticed with what genuine womanly pleasure this woman ran down to the market to purchase greens and other foodstuffs, ever conscious of her role as industrious housewife caring for her charge. If I didn't eat much, she was insulted, and it would have made her deathly unhappy if I had refused to eat at all. In my opinion, a person must at times submit to accepting kindness and generosity—after all, there are times one must submit to their opposite. When I rejected, rather brusquely, all the other good things Frau Scheer was prepared to give me, she would say, "What a wicked man you are," and was dissatisfied with me. The poor woman, she was dreaming! She forgot who she was. She forgot her sad, unlovely existence, her frailty and her melancholy age. She forgot the world's unrelentingness, and if something or other reminded her of this again, her eyes would instantly fill with tears. She rhapsodized like a girl of twenty, and when she was then reminded of her age and all the evil in this world, her face involuntarily assumed an evil aspect: the face of evil, greedy Frau Scheer. After all, her life was coming to an end, and let no one try to tell me that battlefields and other horrors are any more terrifying and horrific than the end of any human existence. All endings are cruel, and every human life is a heroic life, and dying—everywhere, and under no matter what circumstances—is equally bleak, cruel, and sad, and every human being must prepare himself for the poorest and worst exigencies, and every room in which a dead person is laid out is a tragic room, and there was never a human life that lacked tragedy of the most sublime sort.

"I would so dearly love to be born anew, to start living all over again, to be very small and young so as to start life once more from the beginning, but then I would like to live quite differently than before. I would like to be an inconspicuous, poor woman, to be good and gentle and love my fellow human beings so as to be loved by them in return and be welcome everywhere I go. And my joie de vivre should not be of such a sorrowful bent. It should be quite, quite different. My God, I am so unhappy to be dying because I would so love to be walking better paths. You understand, don't you, and you respect me a little, and you care for me a little bit too. Everyone despises and abhors me, mocks me and wishes for bad things to befall me. My great wealth! What should I do with it now, what good comfort does it offer me? I should like to give you a million of your own! But what would I be giving you? I should like to give you far, far more than that. I should like to make you happy, but I can't see with what. I am very fond of you, and that is possibly enough for you, for I noticed long ago that you are easily contented. It isn't possessions that give you joy. You too have honor, and you take meticulous care to preserve it. So let me at least say to you that your presence brings me great joy. I thank you for having been willing to interact with me a little, and for being friendly to me from time to time." She spoke these words to me in her room one night. I didn't quite know what to say in response, and so I drew the conversation to other matters.

I still remember one New Year's Eve when I stood together with Frau Scheer at the open window. Everything outdoors was swathed in thick fog. We were listening to the New Year's bells. The following autumn she fell ill, and the doctors recommended an operation. Forced to make a decision, she entered the clinic from which she never returned. She left no testament. All attempts to look for one turned up nothing. Her estate was divided among her relatives. As for myself, I soon left town. I felt the urge to revisit my distant homeland, the sight of which I'd had to do without for so many years.

1915

THE MILLIONAIRESS

IN HER five-room apartment there lived, all alone, a wealthy lady. I'm saying "lady," but this woman didn't deserve to be called a lady, the poor thing. She ran about all disheveled, and her neighbors referred to her as a Gypsy or witch. Her own person appeared to her to have no value, and she took no pleasure in life. Often she didn't even bother to comb her hair or wash, and on top of this she wore shoddy old clothes, this is how greatly it pleased her to neglect herself. She was wealthy, she might have lived like a queen, but she had no taste for luxury, nor did she have the time. Rich as she was, she was the poorest of women. She had to pass her days and evenings all alone. Not a single person, with the possible exception of Emma, her former maid, kept her company. She was on bad terms with every one of her relatives. She might still get an occasional visit from Mrs. Snubnose, wife of the police commissioner, but otherwise no one came to call. She struck people as repugnant because she walked around looking like a beggar woman; they called her a skinflint, and indeed she was stingy. Stinginess had become a passion of hers. She had no children. And so stinginess became her child. Stinginess is an unattractive child, not a sweet one. Truly not. But a person does have to have something or other to hug and caress. As she sat alone like that in her joyless room in the still of night, this poor rich lady often found herself obliged to weep into her handkerchief. The tears she wept had more honorable intentions toward her than did anyone else. Otherwise this woman was universally hated and betrayed. The pain she felt within her soul was the single upright friend she had. Otherwise she had neither friend nor confidante, nor a son, nor a daughter. In vain did she long for a son who would have comforted her in his childish way. Her living room was not a room for living, it was an office, overloaded with business papers, and in her bedroom stood the iron safe filled with gold and jewels. Verily: a sinister and sad room for a woman to be sleeping in! I made the acquaintance of this woman and found her exceedingly interesting. I told her my life story, and she told me hers. Soon thereafter she died. She left behind several million. Her heirs came and threw themselves upon their inheritance. Poor millionairess! In the city where she lived, there are many, many poor little children who do not even have enough to eat. What a strange world this is we live in.

1914 (?)

A HOMECOMING IN THE SNOW

FOR SEVERAL years I lived there, getting by as best I could. I was in no way lacking in stimuli, encouragement, and the like. At times, to be sure, I suffered greatly, engaged in arduous struggles, but nonetheless always believed there was something lovely about struggling. I would never have wanted things to be different. Everywhere I've lived, I've always found myself from time to time in serious quandaries. Startling quantities of good fortune were never something I longed to receive. Never did I wish to have it better than numerous others. At no time did I attempt to deny to myself that worries have an educational effect and that distress, being disagreeable, a hindrance, strengthens a person's character.

If I make so bold as to remark that during my time there I experienced for the most part no success at all with any of my at least at times ardently pursued endeavors, I am in no way maligning the region of which I speak, for I have no cause to do so. I am assuredly permitted to say that while the favor I found there gave me genuine pleasure, the failures I experienced were never able to sully or take away my sense of joyous equanimity. In the most pleasant way possible, industriousness was demanded of me, and it is only fitting that I openly acknowledge the intelligent, kind people I had the privilege of consorting with, who nobly and plainly drew my attention to matters of the utmost significance. I hope to be giving voice to something that is beyond all doubt universally comprehensible when I declare myself of the opinion that ingratitude is unattractive and at the same time idiotic—indeed it is a curse of the highest order. It was uncommonly satisfying for me—uplifting, even—that several people there, whose estimable images will remain forever fixed in my memory, thought me talented and therefore chose to reiterate their belief again and again that I might be capable of something, and that I was seen as possessing the drive to step out of my own being and onto the brightly lit stage to seek fulfillment in the joyful, magnanimous act of writing.

Perhaps these people I'm remembering thought almost too highly of me in their kindness and amiability—by which, admittedly, I appear to be putting myself down all too vigorously, which would be neither natural nor fitting. Above all else, though, I would like to demonstrate how greatly I aspire to be able to recognize that there is no more desirable pleasure in life than reaping acknowledgment and saying yes to the various benevolent phenomena one has been permitted to see and experience. To comment in any way other than with the greatest meticulousness and reverence on the capitals and squares where the most various meanings and the best achievements of a nation come together from all surrounding regions as if for a grand national assembly must, no doubt, necessarily appear impossible to any cautious thinker.

The thought that I was permitted to swim in such refreshing waters, to actively and convivially—should I be allowed to express myself thus—join in running upon such a racetrack, to live in such appealing and inspiring surrounds, under such powerfully invigorating, often even exhilarating circumstances, to pass a substantial part of my existence so gaily and for the most part so joyfully—this is a thought that should, in my opinion, always put me in a cheerful and also, for propriety's sake, contented state of mind, for there is such a thing as propriety vis-à-vis Heaven and not just mankind, and this is something no person capable of forthright feeling and thought would ever leave entirely out of account.

Having attracted all sorts of notice and acquired the justification to circulate casually among persons worthy of respect by no means assured me, however, of a proper, innocuous income. While laboring with as much vigor as I could muster, I committed errors. Wrestling with ignorance and inability, I came to know my limits and was forced to realize that many things could not be as swiftly accomplished as I would have liked to imagine. Enervation and exhaustion set in. My strength failed me on more than one important occasion. Instead of contenting myself with the lucrative, I ran after unattainable goals, which wasted a great deal of time as well as good courage. Exertions carried out in vain rendered me effectively ill. I destroyed much that I had created with great effort. The more earnestly I longed and strived to put myself on a firm footing, the more clearly I saw myself teetering on the brink. I believe I have never deceived myself particularly in matters of this sort, and since I felt a compulsion to attain a certain tidiness of affairs with regard to my own person, above all to be at one with myself again, I resolved to carefully detach myself from an existence in which I could not place my trust and to return. It seemed to me advisable to bite into insight, which is well known to have a bitter taste. To be sure, I felt and saw the eyes of a beautiful woman looking questioningly at me. This tie, and other ones as well, now had to be shaken off. Slowly I made my way home. Later, I thought, I would be freshly serviceable once more.

On my way home, which struck me as splendid, it was snowing in thick, warm, large flakes. It seemed to me as if I heard homeland-like sounds ringing out from afar. My steps were brisk despite the deep snow through which I was assiduously wading. With every step I took, my shaken trust grew firmer again, which filled me with joy the way a child rejoices. All former things bloomed fragrantly and youthfully in my direction, like roses. It almost appeared to me as if the earth were singing a sweet Christmas melody that was at the same time a melody of spring.

In the darkness a gray, tall figure was suddenly standing there on the road before me. It was a man. How gigantic he seemed to me. "What are you doing standing here?" I asked him. "I am rooted here. What business is it of yours?" he replied.

Leaving behind me this man whom I did not know, who after all surely knew what it was his duty to do, I went on. At times it seemed to me I had wings, though I was working my way forward laboriously enough. Courage and optimism enlivened me on my difficult path, for I was able to tell myself I was heading in the right direction. I looked forward to the future as never before, even though I was making a humble retreat. Yet at the same time I by no means considered myself crushed, rather I had a notion to call myself a conqueror, which then made me laugh. I was not wearing a coat. I considered the snow itself a splendidly warm coat.

Soon I would hear the language of my parents, brothers, and sisters being spoken once more, and I would set foot again upon the dear soil of my native land.

1917

TITLES IN SERIES

J.R. ACKERLEY Hindoo Holiday
J.R. ACKERLEY My Dog Tulip
J.R. ACKERLEY My Father and Myself
J.R. ACKERLEY We Think the World of You
HENRY ADAMS The Jeffersonian Transformation
CÉLESTE ALBARET Monsieur Proust
DANTE ALIGHIERI The Inferno
DANTE ALIGHIERI The New Life
WILLIAM ATTAWAY Blood on the Forge
W.H. AUDEN (EDITOR) The Living Thoughts of Kierkegaard
W.H. AUDEN W.H. Auden's Book of Light Verse
ERICH AUERBACH Dante: Poet of the Secular World
DOROTHY BAKER Cassandra at the Wedding
J.A. BAKER The Peregrine
HONORÉ DE BALZAC The Unknown Masterpiece *and* Gambara
MAX BEERBOHM Seven Men
STEPHEN BENATAR Wish Her Safe at Home
FRANS G. BENGTSSON The Long Ships
ALEXANDER BERKMAN Prison Memoirs of an Anarchist
GEORGES BERNANOS Mouchette
ADOLFO BIOY CASARES Asleep in the Sun
ADOLFO BIOY CASARES The Invention of Morel
CAROLINE BLACKWOOD Corrigan
CAROLINE BLACKWOOD Great Granny Webster
NICOLAS BOUVIER The Way of the World
MALCOLM BRALY On the Yard
MILLEN BRAND The Outward Room
JOHN HORNE BURNS The Gallery
ROBERT BURTON The Anatomy of Melancholy
CAMARA LAYE The Radiance of the King
GIROLAMO CARDANO The Book of My Life
DON CARPENTER Hard Rain Falling
J.L. CARR A Month in the Country
BLAISE CENDRARS Moravagine
EILEEN CHANG Love in a Fallen City
UPAMANYU CHATTERJEE English, August: An Indian Story
NIRAD C. CHAUDHURI The Autobiography of an Unknown Indian
ANTON CHEKHOV Peasants and Other Stories
RICHARD COBB Paris and Elsewhere
COLETTE The Pure and the Impure
JOHN COLLIER Fancies and Goodnights
CARLO COLLODI The Adventures of Pinocchio
IVY COMPTON-BURNETT A House and Its Head
IVY COMPTON-BURNETT Manservant and Maidservant
BARBARA COMYNS The Vet's Daughter
EVAN S. CONNELL The Diary of a Rapist
ALBERT COSSERY The Jokers
ALBERT COSSERY Proud Beggars
HAROLD CRUSE The Crisis of the Negro Intellectual
ASTOLPHE DE CUSTINE Letters from Russia

For a complete list of titles, visit www.nyrb.com or write to:
Catalog Requests, NYRB, 435 Hudson Street, New York, NY 10014

GREGOR VON REZZORI Memoirs of an Anti-Semite
GREGOR VON REZZORI The Snows of Yesteryear: Portraits for an Autobiography
TIM ROBINSON Stones of Aran: Labyrinth
TIM ROBINSON Stones of Aran: Pilgrimage
MILTON ROKEACH The Three Christs of Ypsilanti
FR. ROLFE Hadrian the Seventh
GILLIAN ROSE Love's Work
WILLIAM ROUGHEAD Classic Crimes
CONSTANCE ROURKE American Humor: A Study of the National Character
TAYEB SALIH Season of Migration to the North
TAYEB SALIH The Wedding of Zein
GERSHOM SCHOLEM Walter Benjamin: The Story of a Friendship
DANIEL PAUL SCHREBER Memoirs of My Nervous Illness
JAMES SCHUYLER Alfred and Guinevere
JAMES SCHUYLER What's for Dinner?
LEONARDO SCIASCIA The Day of the Owl
LEONARDO SCIASCIA Equal Danger
LEONARDO SCIASCIA The Moro Affair
LEONARDO SCIASCIA To Each His Own
LEONARDO SCIASCIA The Wine-Dark Sea
VICTOR SEGALEN René Leys
PHILIPE-PAUL DE SÉGUR Defeat: Napoleon's Russian Campaign
VICTOR SERGE The Case of Comrade Tulayev
VICTOR SERGE Conquered City
VICTOR SERGE Unforgiving Years
SHCHEDRIN The Golovlyov Family
GEORGES SIMENON Act of Passion
GEORGES SIMENON Dirty Snow
GEORGES SIMENON The Engagement
GEORGES SIMENON The Man Who Watched Trains Go By
GEORGES SIMENON Monsieur Monde Vanishes
GEORGES SIMENON Pedigree
GEORGES SIMENON Red Lights
GEORGES SIMENON The Strangers in the House
GEORGES SIMENON Three Bedrooms in Manhattan
GEORGES SIMENON Tropic Moon
GEORGES SIMENON The Widow
CHARLES SIMIC Dime-Store Alchemy: The Art of Joseph Cornell
MAY SINCLAIR Mary Olivier: A Life
TESS SLESINGER The Unpossessed: A Novel of the Thirties
VLADIMIR SOROKIN Ice Trilogy
VLADIMIR SOROKIN The Queue
DAVID STACTON The Judges of the Secret Court
JEAN STAFFORD The Mountain Lion
CHRISTINA STEAD Letty Fox: Her Luck
GEORGE R. STEWART Names on the Land
STENDHAL The Life of Henry Brulard
ADALBERT STIFTER Rock Crystal
THEODOR STORM The Rider on the White Horse
JEAN STROUSE Alice James: A Biography
HOWARD STURGIS Belchamber
ITALO SVEVO As a Man Grows Older
HARVEY SWADOS Nights in the Gardens of Brooklyn